ANOTHER STORY

Women and
The Falklands War

by

Jean Carr

Introduction by Jane Ewart-Biggs

HAMISH HAMILTON LONDON

To Louis and Mum

First published in Great Britain 1984
by Hamish Hamilton Ltd
Garden House 57–59 Long Acre London WC2E 9JZ

Copyright © 1984 by Jean Carr

British Library Cataloguing in Publication Data

Carr, Jean
   Another story.
   1. Falkland Islands War, 1982—Social aspects—Great Britain
   2. Soldiers—Great Britain—Family relationships—History—
   20th century
   I. Title
   355.2'2'0941   F3031.5

ISBN 0–241–11391–1
ISBN 0–241–11354–7 pbk

Typeset by Katerprint Co. Ltd, Oxford
Printed in Great Britain by
Billing & Sons Ltd, Worcester

Contents

Introduction

Another Story is well named. Jean Carr's account shows us the reverse side of the Falklands coin. She spells out fundamental truths which set the glamourised public view of the Falklands conflict against the tragic human aftermath. It is a disturbing story, for the author describes the lack of humanity, confusion and poor organisation in dealing with the needs of the Servicemen's families once the battle was over. As Jean Carr says: 'It is appalling that a system that could so rapidly mobilise a twenty-eight thousand strong task force was so incapable of dealing with the consequences of such a brief, bitter war.'

The chapter titles of Jean Carr's human and moving book give – very clearly – the sequence of events in the lives of the Servicemen's families. First came the hasty departure of the young warriors – the average age of the soldiers was only nineteen years. This, in many cases, was followed by a total lack of news for the families waiting anxiously at home. But when the news did come – sometimes of death and injury – it was given to the wives and families with lack of sensitivity and little thought for their feelings. The descriptions of the type and scale of physical injuries inflicted by modern weaponry were heartrending; as were the references to other scars left by war, those left on the minds of combatants. 'People can see when a man has lost an arm or a leg, but nobody can see what a war does to a man's mind.'

The narrative goes on to focus on the sense of grievance felt by the wives and families of the wounded men at the failure of the government to make adequate provision for them. It seemed to them that – whilst the Prime Minister was quick enough in making use of their husbands, sweethearts and sons to fight a war from which she gained considerable political capital – she then ducked her financial obligations to the relatives. Instead the government took advantage of the South Atlantic Fund set up through the generosity of ordinary people. But the relatives' gratitude for this was tempered by the fact that the mismanagement of the Fund, together with our outdated Charity Law, prevented help being given initially when the young widows and families were in most need.

Intermingled in her narrative, the author brings out some basic facts about the changing attitudes and life patterns of Service wives. She points out how, in line with modern trends among all women, the Service wife also seeks a certain autonomy, a job of her own and indeed no longer regards her husband's profession as sacrosanct. For example, in days gone by, how many Sergeant's wives would have said, as Marica McKay did: 'Governments should go on talking for as long as possible before using guns'? But in spite of her efforts to achieve this degree of independence, as Jean Carr reveals, there is a deep sense of isolation suffered by a Service widow when she is cut off from both the institution and the community of which she has been such an integral part. One of the wives put it in unequivocal terms: 'Wives and families are excess baggage and the only interest the Service have in you is what your husband does. If you lose him you not only lose your status, but your way of life and, eventually, your home if you live in married quarters.'

I can myself identify with much that has been said in this book. Although, of course, the circumstances of losing my Diplomat husband through terrorist action made my case very different from theirs, nevertheless I too have suffered from the implacable nature of the 'system'. For a Diplomatic Service widow also finds herself instantly cut off from the institution – and freemasonry – of which she has been a devoted member. (I remember even crossing out all the future entries in my diary, as each one had been connected to the Diplomatic profession.) So this made me feel very close to the wives who spoke of the problems of building a new life from scratch, everything from the former having disappeared. And, although, as they did, I benefited so much from people's kindness and concern, nevertheless I too have encountered and suffered from the Anglo-Saxon inhibition about death and bereavement. It is as if death is taboo to some of the English and should be pushed under the carpet. I called it the 'leprosy syndrome', for sometimes people crossed to the other side of the road when they saw me coming to avoid having to find something to say. I supposed they hoped they could make the whole distasteful thing disappear. As one of the widows in *Another Story* remarked, people had asked if she felt 'better' as if widowhood was a minor illness from which she should make every effort to recover. But she and I and many others know that bereavement brings with it life's greatest crisis and the survivor of a marriage will never entirely 'get over it'.

I also felt a bond with her when she said she wondered if she would always be known as the Falklands War widow, rather than a person in her own right, 'whoever that might be'. My label was – and sometimes still is – 'the murdered envoy's widow', and I often feel that whilst I have worked so hard to reconstruct and recreate a life to fill the void the label does nothing but serve as a reminder of the negative and cruel act.

Reading *Another Story* took me full circle from when I listened on my car radio to the debates on the Falklands crisis in both Houses of Parliament on the morning of Saturday 3 April, 1982. I should, in fact, have been taking part in the Lords Debate myself but, as is often the case these days, my parliamentary and maternal obligations clashed; with the final decision on this occasion to proceed with a planned visit to Stratford-on-Avon with my younger daughter to see a performance of *Macbeth*. As we drove along, I listened with mounting horror to the note of bellicosity and of wounded national pride in the voices of the majority of the speakers. I could hardly believe the emotive language used. 'The government must now prove by deeds . . . to ensure that foul and brutal aggression does not succeed in our world. . . .' Another speaker went even further: '. . . the very thought that our people, 1,800 people of British blood and bone, could be left in the hands of such criminals is enough to make any normal Englishman's blood boil – and the blood of Scotsmen and Welshmen boil too.'

At lunch time, Kate and I stopped for a picnic down a grassy land just beyond Oxford, but the voices on the radio carried on relentlessly. Just before two o'clock, the Secretary of State for Defence wound up the debate: '. . . from next Monday, the Royal Navy will put to sea in wartime order and with wartime stock and weapons. That force will include the carriers HMS *Invincible* and HMS *Hermes*, the assault ship HMS *Fearless* and a number of destroyers and frigates armed with anti-surface and anti-air missiles together with afloat support. A strong force of Royal Marine commandos and a large number of Sea Harriers and anti-submarine and troop-carrying helicopters will also be embarked . . .' The end of our sandwiches coincided with Britain being at war. I was dumbfounded. The very size of the decision taken by the government – with all-Party support in Parliament – was too much to absorb all at once.

I wondered if, had I been at the Debate, I would have found the courage to voice my doubts in such a welter of certitude. Even under normal circumstances I am reticent about discussing military and defence issues as, with an overwhelming repugnance for violence and conflict, it is difficult to find common ground for objective argument. I realise that God – for his own purposes – succeeds in reconciling the need for both war and peace, but my own bias is so heavily weighted on the side of negotiation, compromise and conciliation that I cannot achieve His balance. I even go as far as regarding any justification for revenge and retribution as un-Christian.

So, driving through the lovely peaceful countryside, I feared I might have funked speaking out against the military option and in favour of continued negotiation and diplomatic pressure. I knew that any practical arguments based on the technical difficulties, the risk to life, the expenditure of funds so badly needed for home policies the eventual failure to find a long-term political solution, etc., would have borne no weight against those arguing from wounded national pride. Moreover, I realised dissenters would be regarded as traitors once the task force had sailed and our men's lives had been put at risk. And then I was suddenly reminded of the old nursery story about the dishonest tailors who made imaginary clothes for the King, claiming that their magical quality rendered them visible only to people who were intelligent. The King, thus attired, paraded before his people who were silent and admiring; until, suddenly, the voice of a small child rang out: 'But the King hasn't got any clothes on.' His subjects then turned against him and reviled him. Did we not now need the voice of a child to cry out loud and clear – as the task force sailed off – 'But is it really worth it?'

It is important to recognise that the voices of the widows, wives and families used by Jean Carr to tell *Another Story* were not raised only in criticism. They also expressed wholehearted admiration and gratitude for the medical expertise given to their wounded. They spoke of the comfort they drew from the concern and help coming from the ordinary people of Britain; not only those who gave so generously to the Fund but also all those who out of a sense of compassion came to their rescue in different ways. So, although the author brings unequivocal proof of the fearful human consequences of modern war and reveals society's failure to mount a successful rescue operation for its survivors, nevertheless, to me, the underlying theme of *Another Story* is about two levels of courage. The courage of those who set off unquestioningly to uphold the principle of international law, risking death or injury in the cause. And the courage of the women who waited at home; some of whom eventually were faced with the struggle of continuing their lives alone, and others with the task of supporting their physically or mentally injured husband or son in his fight to recovery. We must salute them all.

Jane Ewart-Biggs
June, 1984

Author's Preface

In the Spring of 1982 the departure of a task force to do battle with Argentine invaders on some South Atlantic islands seemed as unreal to me as it did to many of the Servicemen summoned to war. For someone like myself, born after the Second World War and familiar with debates on nuclear disarmament, the prospect of British troops being killed in naval skirmishes and trench warfare seemed absurd. Rear Admiral Woodward's motley armada was just a bluff, a show of strength – until the sinking of the *Belgrano* and the rapid reprisal on the *Sheffield*.

As a feature writer on the *Sunday Mirror*, I had a professional interest in the media coverage of the Falklands War, although the reports in my paper, like the majority in Fleet Street, were written almost exclusively by political and foreign editors, newsroom staff, and pooled despatches from male journalists with the task force. As I scanned all the papers, and flicked from one television channel to another, I wondered what the Servicemen's families must have thought, when there were so many contradictory and speculative stories that it was sometimes impossible to separate fact from fiction.

I did not know anyone in the Services, never mind the task force, and the Armed Forces were a completely alien world. Two or three times that Spring and early Summer I passed through Plymouth on the way to my mother's home in Cornwall. The Tamar estuary and Devonport dockyard, usually busy with Royal Navy vessels, were deserted. The city's shopping centre and the Hoe, from which Sir Francis Drake had watched the approaching Spanish Armada, had none of the crowds I was familiar with when I had worked there as a journalist on the local *Sunday Independent*. Over 12,000 Servicemen from the Plymouth area had gone to the Falklands – this really was a community at war and, for the first time, I became aware of what their families must be going through. After the troops landed in the Falklands, the war's casualty figures rose and my requests to the Ministry of Defence to try and find out what was happening to the families of the dead and injured were turned down. It was adamant: no one wanted to be interviewed.

The domestic impact of the war was not the sort of situation that could be covered by ringing the door bells of strangers; such a foot-in-the-door approach to the bereaved would have met with rebuffs, and legitimate criticism from the Services themselves. Instead, I talked to friends in the West Country; they introduced me to Service personnel who agreed to act as intermediaries and contact a few families on my behalf. This method guaranteed the families' anonymity if they did not want to be interviewed, and gave them time to consider the request.

My initial introductions and interviews had a snow-balling effect, as more and more Service families contacted *me* with their stories. The families of the war-wounded were particularly anxious about their future and what the Services, the South Atlantic Fund and the government intended to do for them. My inquiries on their behalf were met with the same suspicion and hostility as my earlier requests for interviews. It did not take long to find out why.

The government compensation for medically discharged war-wounded Servicemen was scandalously inadequate. The successful campaign I started on the *Sunday Mirror* resulted in compensation to the Falkland veterans from the £16 million South Atlantic Fund on the same scale as that awarded Servicemen injured in Northern Ireland by the Criminal Injuries Compensation Board. The campaign flushed out attitudes within the Armed Forces and Service charities, completely out-of-date with the expectations of a non-conscript generation who had grown up in a Welfare State.

Every story I wrote led to more Service families all over Britain writing and telephoning me. The majority of letters and calls came from women, because the Queen's Regulations forbade their men publicly to criticise the Services or the government. The Regulations, which govern the conduct of the Armed Forces, mean that Servicemen may not speak to the media without the permission of their commanding officers, and then they may speak only about matters of fact, and not give their personal opinions. All press inquiries must be handled by public relations staff, either at the Ministry of Defence or within the relevant Service. But the Regulations could not silence a generation of women who were articulate, aware of their rights, and eager to secure the best possible future for their children and their men. Many were in their early and mid-thirties, the same age-group as myself, and I could sympathise with their feelings about an all-male military hierarchy which seemed so out of touch with the social changes that have taken place in our lives. The Falklands War was soon forgotten by the media and the public, but for these women, who were adjusting to the domestic aftermath, the war was something that will be with them and their families for the rest of their lives.

By the end of 1982 I had met a number of women – widows, wives and mothers – who were angry and confused about the purpose of the war and, after their men had been killed or injured, the attitudes of the Armed Forces and a government led by Britain's first woman Prime Minister. The war had revealed aspects of the Services that would only have become apparent during such a large-scale conflict. But the impact on the women I knew – and still keep in touch with – really needed the perspective of time. It was not until a year later, and largely at their suggestion, that I decided to record their stories, aware that other people's experiences could have been different.

This book is based on families I have known since the Summer of 1982 and forty additional interviews with widows, wives and mothers. It is not a history book, a war correspondent's diary, or a political analysis. It is *Another Story*, the story of women caught up in a totally unexpected conflict and how it affected their lives, and what they now feel about the Falklands War.

It reveals how women have little more than a social role in the rigid rank structure of Service life; how widows lose not only their husbands but a way of life totally different from civvy street; how the Service charities, who conduct their business like Victorian alms-givers, failed to respond to the immediate needs of the war-wounded; and how the secrecy and chauvinism of the Armed Forces was exposed by women speaking out for themselves – and their men.

It is very much their story, written without the cooperation of the Ministry of Defence, the Armed Forces, or the secretary of the South Atlantic Fund, who once referred to me as 'that interfering woman'.

Another Story is a side of war too often ignored, and too soon forgotten by those who make war.

J.C.
April, 1984

CHAPTER ONE:

Called to War

'We always believed that should there ever be another war it would be The Big One, all or nothing.' Widow Caroline Hailwood.

On the morning he left home, SAS Sergeant Major Lawrence 'Lofty' Gallagher stood in the middle of his sitting room rubbing his hands.

Three days earlier the Argentines had occupied the Falklands and at Hereford, the home base of the Special Air Service, Gallagher's D Squadron had spent the weekend on standby. In the dawn of that April Monday in 1982 as he prepared to leave for RAF Brize Norton and a flight to Ascension Island, Lawrence Gallagher, a thirty-seven-year-old veteran of covert global skirmishes and holder of the British Empire Medal for service in Northern Ireland, was really excited. This was the Real Thing. 'We are going to win medals here,' he told his wife. Lynda Gallagher was more preoccupied with the probability of being newly pregnant with their third child. After seven years of marriage she was familiar with hasty departures for unknown destinations; within a fortnight of their wedding Lawrence had gone abroad for five months and, like generations of Service wives, she was left with just another British Forces post office box number to write to. Lynda says her husband was 'a soldier through and through'. She knew there was never a chance of changing his mind about the Army he had joined as a fifteen-year-old boy soldier, the only alternative to the local pit in the Yorkshire coal-mining village where he was born. In their modern semi-detached home, Lawrence Gallagher had told his wife only about the funny, sometimes ribald things that had happened to him, and she had never worried when he went away. She told me: 'The SAS are the best. I knew Lawrence would be all right. I never once thought he would not come back.'

D Squadron's anonymous flight from RAF Brize Norton was in keeping with the legendary secrecy of the SAS; in contrast was the carnival euphoria of quayside farewells for the armada embarking from Portsmouth, Plymouth and Southampton as the task force sailed for the South Atlantic.

Families of the crew of HMS *Sheffield* felt doubly cheated when they saw television and newspaper pictures of wives, mothers and girlfriends lining docksides and south coast headlands. The *Sheffield*, a Type 42 destroyer, had been on its way home after nearly five months at sea but instead of leaving Gibraltar for Portsmouth it was diverted south.

When Maureen Emly first heard of the change of plan on her local Radio Victory she was upset and angry. In mid-March her husband Richard, a Royal Navy Sub Lieutenant, had telephoned her from Athens where the *Sheffield* had berthed for a week's shore leave after four months in the Gulf. They were scheduled to dock at Portsmouth on 6 April, but Richard Emly could not wait to see his wife and hear the latest news of their six-year-old son Matthew. Maureen flew to Greece with other wives who had received similar homesick calls.

The *Sheffield* was Richard Emly's first ship as a newly commissioned officer who had worked his way up the ranks after joining the Navy at fifteen. A handsome, clever and ambitious electronics specialist, Sub Lieutenant Emly had recently applied for a prestige Royal Navy posting in Washington, America. In his wife's handbag that April weekend was a yellow pass to get into Portsmouth dockyard to meet his ship. On Saturday 3 April Maureen listened to the live radio broadcast of the House of Commons emergency debate on the Falklands and when Margaret Thatcher spoke of sending a task force to the South Atlantic it did not cross her mind that, after five months at sea, the *Sheffield* would go too. The next day came the local radio announcement that the ship was on its way to the Falklands. Maureen remembers how: 'Everyone tried to get a telephone call through to the boat to talk to the men to see what was happening. We were told the ship was not in communication, that they could not talk to us. There was a lot of bitterness that no one had bothered to let us know, to hear it on the radio like that was shocking.'

In fact the news of the *Sheffield*'s departure for the South Atlantic was already two days old. There is no reason, strategic or otherwise, why the families preparing for the *Sheffield*'s homecoming were not told earlier of the change of plan: Margaret Thatcher had announced that a task force was being despatched, notice boards at British Rail and London tube stations displayed urgently chalked messages recalling Servicemen to their barracks, and telephones shrilled summonses in the night.

Forgetting to tell the *Sheffield* families was the first crack in the system: it could mobilise 28,000 men and women within a matter of days but it could not handle the disruptive effects of war on the home front.

Caroline Hailwood was at home in Farnborough, Hants, with her baby son Jim when her husband Christopher telephoned on Saturday at midnight. Christopher was in Plymouth. Caroline says: 'He was in a hell of a state. He said they had been called back from Norway a week early and they were going to the Falklands. I drove to Plymouth on Sunday and when I went to the docks to see him there were these huge Royal Marines everywhere with their guns spoiling for battle. In the middle was Chris, who wasn't much taller than me, looking very lost and upset, and he cried when he saw the baby. It was totally unreal, like an old news reel; the dockyard was bristling with equipment for a D-Day type landing. Chris never joined the Royal Fleet Auxiliary to go to war, he was a civil servant employed by the Ministry of Defence. We always believed that should there ever be another war it would be THE BIG ONE – all or nothing.'

Christopher, a chief engineer in the RFA, had been back at sea for a fortnight after three months' shore leave taken to coincide with the birth of their first child on Christmas Eve. Before Jim was born Christopher had worked on the landing ship *Sir Lancelot* on a rota of six months at sea with occasional weekends at home, and three months ashore. After his son's birth he asked to be transferred to the Southampton-based sister ship the *Sir Galahad*, so that he could go home every weekend. Caroline, a school teacher, told me: 'He loved his work but after those twelve weeks at home with our new baby he did not think he could cope with being separated from Jim for months on end. We were very lucky to have that time together as a family, it was bliss. I was home on maternity leave and we were planning the renovations for a house we had just bought.' During that shore leave Christopher Hailwood was offered a job at Sulzer Bros, a local firm that makes ships' engines and turbines. It was an open offer and he promised his wife he would consider it as a future alternative to being at sea.

Caroline and Christopher were in their mid-twenties, and the Second World War was even more remote to them than to those who had grown up in the Sixties and the Cold War. Caroline was a baby when National Service ended in 1962; she and her contemporaries knew little or nothing of the Armed Forces. Theirs was a generation more familiar with debates on the siting of Cruise missiles; they assumed future global confrontations would be nuclear. Christopher Hailwood was a non-combatant, and his wife's incredulity that her husband should be caught up in preparations for a conventional war was understandable. Her feelings were shared by many Service families, who were also confused.

When seventeen-year-old Jason Burt of the 3rd Battalion Parachute Regiment telephoned his mum to say he was sailing on the *Canberra* to the Falklands, she told him to give her a call when he got there and reverse the charge if he was short of change. Theresa Burt remembers: 'Jason couldn't stop laughing. Just before the pips he said to get Ann, a school teacher friend of ours, to tell us where it was.'

Jason and his fellow soldiers were among some 3,000 military personnel aboard the liner *Canberra*, requisitioned from Cunard by the Ministry of Defence when she docked at Southampton from a Mediterranean cruise. Within days the 45,000 ton vessel had been refitted as a troopship, her main swimming pool covered with steel plates to make a helicopter pad. She left for the South Atlantic on Good Friday, 9 April, just a week after the Argentines had invaded the Falklands, during which the build-up for Operation Corporate, the military name for the South Atlantic campaign, had dominated the news.

In spite of the newspaper and television coverage the complexities of why Britain should be going to war with a South American dictator over a group of islands substantially owned by a private trading company were lost on families whose husbands and sons expected the only action in their Service lives to be on the streets of Ulster, an unpleasant task they regarded more as a policing operation than war. Jason Burt was not allowed to serve in Northern Ireland until he was eighteen. Three months before that birthday he was sent to the Falklands. Not once did his parents imagine their child – still a boy – would be involved in hand-to-hand trench warfare, reminiscent of the First World War.

The average age of the Soldier embarking for the South Atlantic was nineteen. Most had joined the Forces to avoid dole queues, get away from home, learn a trade, or escape the boredom of mundane jobs; some teenage Welsh Guardsmen were in the tradition of young men 'serving time' with a family regiment, while the Parachute Regiment and the Royal Marines recruit those drawn by the challenge of their reputations for professionalism and toughness. The rookies of the 1980s are trained by career soldiers for whom the Armed Forces had become a very competitive profession, and for whom promotion often meant learning new skills in the increasingly computerised technology of nuclear warfare. The possibility of a conventional war, even on a limited scale, rated little attention in their theoretical war games.

For many young men in the Eighties, staying on in the Forces is preferable to the problems of recession in civvy street and possible unemployment. The uniforms, regimental traditions and rivalries, the camaraderie of an all-male society, the social life of barracks and mess rooms, still hold a certain glamour. Their wives look forward to the few overseas postings left, Berlin being the most popular; their children can get subsidised fees at private schools; a home always goes with the job, sometimes on attractive modern estates like those at Pirbright, Surrey, or sometimes smart Service flats in London's Knightsbridge and Chelsea barracks.

Apart from the times they are separated from their families by Northern Ireland duties, overseas tours like Belize, and training courses, many soldiers keep office hours and lead civilian-style lives at home with their families. Many young wives with school-age children go out to work; they like to have their own jobs and they want to help buy a family home of their own. Once settled in their own houses, fewer wives move to new postings with their husbands. They are reluctant to interrupt their children's schooling and, in some cases, their own careers. This new generation of young Service wives pays amused lip service to the formalities of rank and file. They tend to regard their men's work as 'just another job' and, while respecting their husbands' dedication, try to lead their own lives. That their husbands should be involved in a war halfway across the world in defence of a British sheep farming community of less than two thousand people was utterly unforeseen.

At the end of that first week of the Argentine occupation the majority of the Armed Forces families were prepared to accept the principle behind sending a task force to the Falklands. By and large they endorsed Margaret Thatcher's sentiments: 'The people of the Falkland Islands have the right to live in peace, to choose their own way of life, and to determine their own allegiance.' But few of the families, or their men, really thought that the hastily assembled and motley armada of converted liners, North Sea ferries, and the remnants of a much pruned Royal Navy that set sail that Spring would ever do battle. They never once imagined the D-Day style landing of their men eight thousand miles away on a remote group of islands, where British sovereignty is still being debated. Wives like Lynda Gallagher thought the Prime Minister's sabre rattling would send the invaders scuttling for home, or force a diplomatic solution. She could not believe her husband's anticipation that this could be the Real Thing and remembers thinking: 'It was just another exercise. They would come back before they were anywhere near the Falklands.' To Maureen Emly it was unthinkable that the *Sheffield* and her husband would be engaged in naval warfare; 'Richard was in the Royal

Navy, or what was left of it after all the defence cuts, and the only real role for those ships other than NATO commitments was the diplomatic one of sailing around showing the British flag.'

But the large-scale mobilisation made some Servicemen very uneasy. They tried to hide their fears from their families in their last-minute telephone calls, and hurried explanations to wives on how to handle their affairs, 'just in case something happened', which only increased the women's apprehension.

For the first time in their twelve-year marriage Sergeant Andy Evans, a thirty-three-year-old Royal Marine helicopter pilot from 3 Commando Brigade Air Squadron, told his wife about the financial arrangements should anything happen to him. June Evans sat listening in the sitting room of their home in the Cornish village of Landrake, as her husband told her he had made a will and itemised the insurance policy on the house they had moved to the previous Spring, their first own home after years in Service quarters. She felt panic knotting her stomach, a feeling that would stay with her.

For almost a week June said 'goodbye' each morning before leaving for her job as a clerical officer at Devonport dockyard, and in the evening found Andy still at home. Her husband spent the last few days panelling the stairs, and the sitting room smelt of paint from the newly painted door and half-done window frame; the paint pot and brush still stood on the sill. It was a job his wife would refuse to let anyone finish for over a year.

Across the Tamar estuary that divides Cornwall from the Plymouth naval dockyards Sue Enefer had put her two daughters, Donna, aged eight, and Lisa, eleven years old, to bed when her Royal Marine husband, Sergeant Roger Enefer, stationed with 45 Commando in Arbroath, Scotland, telephoned. He had joined 45 on 9 March 1982 after two years as a works liaison officer at the Marines training centre in Lympstone, Devon. Sergeant Enefer had spent a brief twenty-four hours of his week's leave at his Plymouth home before being recalled to barracks on 2 April. The night before he left for the Falklands he phoned and asked to speak to the children who were asleep. Sue says: 'He had never done that before going away. I woke them and when Donna told her father she loved him he cried. He told me that if anything happened Dave my brother-in-law would sort everything out. He had done eleven tours in Northern Ireland and not once spoken like that.'

During the Easter school holidays the largest British fleet since the Suez crisis in 1956 continued to be assembled – in total over 100 Royal Navy and requisitioned merchant vessels, including Cunard's 14,946 ton-container ship *Atlantic Conveyor*, which left Devonport dockyard the third week in April.

The *Conveyor*'s master was Captain Ian North, a bearded veteran seafarer affectionately known as Captain Birdseye. His chief mechanic was forty-eight-year-old Frank Foulkes from Kirkham, Lancashire, who had joined the Royal Navy as a fifteen-year-old, left for a spell ashore when his six children were growing up, then returned to sea to work as a mechanic for Cunard. He and his wife Dorothy had known each other since their schooldays. They had met in her parents' Blackpool amusement arcade, and married when both were nineteen. Frank, a tall, powerfully built man who boxed for the Royal Navy, and Dorothy, with her Junoesque figure and dark good looks, were a popular couple whose lives centred around their five daughters and son David. Frank had worked on the *Conveyor* for six years on a regular trans-Atlantic cargo run of nine weeks at sea and three weeks at home.

Dorothy Foulkes had years ago accepted that her husband's first love was the sea: 'It made him happy and he earned good money with Cunard. I never saw any danger in him being in merchant shipping especially on a vessel as big as the *Conveyor*, he was as safe as houses.' Frank particularly enjoyed working with the same small crew of twenty or so men without the formality of ranks and the rule-book discipline of the Royal Navy. He vetoed Cunard's passenger liners because as an officer he was expected to dress in 'whites' and take dinner with the passengers. On the *Conveyor* he had spent a lot of effort making his cabin a 'home from home', and as soon as the ship docked in Liverpool was straight ashore and back to his family. His wife admits to spending all the time he was away preparing for him to come home, stocking up the freezer with her home cooking and doing the minimum of housework

8

once he walked through the front door. Their youngest three daughters' love for horses prompted him to learn how to ride and on one shore leave, with characteristic enthusiasm, he bought himself a horse and two ponies for Elizabeth, who was then fifteen, Victoria, age eleven, and Charlotte, eight. The Foulkes had started to make plans for Frank's retirement from Cunard and with her usual elan Dorothy had taken a school leavers' catering course at a local college and temporarily managed a small cake shop, in preparation for helping her husband run a country pub: 'Something we hoped to buy to keep us busy in our old age and where Frank could keep his horse.'

On April 13 Petty Officer Foulkes was on leave when Cunard's London office crew superintendent phoned him to say: 'Your ship is sailing in the morning. You know where she is going. Are you going with her?' Dorothy Foulkes says her husband did not hesitate. He left the next day.

They sailed from Liverpool to Devonport dockyard to be refitted. The *Atlantic Conveyor* cargo would include the Harriers the aircraft carriers *Invincible* and *Hermes* had been unable to accommodate; a mobile landing strip so the planes could operate from shore; four giant twin-rotor Chinook helicopters capable of lifting up to eighty troops or ten tons of supplies; and so many tents that Frank Foulkes, in a letter to his wife, said he did not think the Falklands were big enough to take them all. He also told her there was so much ammunition on board that if anything hit them it would be one Big Bang, but as they had not been fitted with a defence system he assumed they would unload their cargo at Ascension Island and stay outside the combat zone. Before leaving Devonport he phoned home to say how delighted he was to be in 'mixed' ships' company with the Royal Air Force and Royal Navy personnel on board. Dorothy remembers: 'He was so excited about the Royal Navy being on the *Conveyor*, he was back in his second youth.'

Among the Royal Navy crew drafted to the *Conveyor* was Chief Petty Officer Edmund Flanagan. Edmund, who had been in the Royal Navy for twenty-two years, had that February been posted from Chatham dockyard to HMS *Neptune*, Faslane, Scotland. His wife Anita, a state registered nurse, had decided to stay in their married quarters in Rainham, where two of their four children were still at school, and she could continue her night nursing job at a local psychiatric hospital. Edmund was thirty-seven. In his full dress uniform, and with his carefully trimmed beard, looking every inch a Royal Navy officer, he was a Writer, a job which his wife in her down-to-earth way describes as 'a glorified clerk, in charge of all the ship's company's paperwork'. He had been shore-based since May 1981, and with defence cuts scheduled to hit the Royal Navy more than other Services, he did not rate too highly his chances of returning to sea before his scheduled retirement in June 1984, although that Easter he told his wife he had decided to sign on for another five years.

Edmund was still on leave when the phone rang at 4 pm on 14 April recalling him to Scotland. His wife, a caring, capable woman, is not given to panic or a vivid imagination. But on the day her husband left their Rainham home she had a feeling he would not return. His last words were: 'Don't worry. We Writers have a reputation for walking on water.' He travelled to Scotland only to be sent five days later to Plymouth, from where he phoned home to say because of strict security he could not tell her which ship he was on but she could contact him by calling the dockyard and asking for Naval Party 1840. Anita was amused when her call was transferred to Naval Party 1840 and someone answered 'Atlantic Conveyor'. She describes her feelings after the ship left as 'just blind fear'.

There were thirteen Naval households on Anita Flanagan's estate and five of them had men in the task force. From being on nodding terms, the women began to seek each other out. They sat together listening to and watching the news bulletins, sometimes cooking communal meals, baby-sitting and shopping for each other, anything rather than be alone with their thoughts. Sue Enefer, whose Royal Marine husband Roger had been among the first to leave, described to me how she spent her days waiting for news: 'I would go from the half past the hour news headlines on the radio to the TV news and back again just trying to catch everything. It must have been terrible for the children.' The task force families scoured the newspapers for clues as to where their men might be. They had no idea what was really happening to them.

At the beginning, the war was a Naval operation and the Royal Navy had not handled such a situation since the Second World War. The fleet commander, Rear Admiral John 'Sandy' Woodward, plucked from his desk job in Whitehall, had little idea how to deal with a press clamouring for information. Newspaper and television programme editors were finding it as difficult as their readers and viewers to ferret out facts about Operation Corporate. Woodward, after the retaking of South Georgia on 25 April, in true Popeye the Sailor fashion, told a task force journalist: 'This is the run up to the big match which, in my view, should be a walkover.' His remarks were as inappropriate and premature as Margaret Thatcher's shouts of 'Rejoice, just rejoice', from the steps of Downing Street after John Nott's hesitant announcement of the South Georgia reoccupation to waiting press men.

At first the Fleet Headquarters at Northwood did not want any journalists to sail with the task force, an attitude very much in keeping with the complete absence of discussion on the role of the media in the training of officers at the Royal Navy's Dartmouth college. Even the Ministry of Defence were aghast at Northwood's blind disregard of media requests for coverage in an age when TV cameras had filmed in the middle of the battlefields of Vietnam, Israel and Iran – let alone on-the-spot reports from Ulster, often with the complete cooperation of the British Army. Media expectations for similar facilities to report the Falklands War were thwarted at home, initially by the hostility at Northwood, later by censorship and news management at the Ministry of Defence, and in the South Atlantic by the technical problems of transmitting satellite pictures from warships moving at speed and the obstruction of some Service personnel in charge of communications.

Hard news gave way to speculation, rumour, inaccuracy and endless circular discussion of the issues not the facts. This added to the general feeling of unreality and unease among the task force families. There was saturation television coverage on various diplomatic moves, emergency debates of the United Nations, studio discussions with retired senior Service personnel hovering over scale models of battleships, eager to predict the possible military moves, but nowhere was there a hint of what was really happening in the South Atlantic. Both the BBC and ITN compensated for the lack of task force pictures with on-the-spot commentary from Chile, Uruguay and Argentina, including film of Argentines discussing the merits of the war, interviews that angered some viewers and led to accusations of unpatriotic bias. ITN's *News At Ten* introduced a Falklands Extra, BBC's *Newsnight* concentrated on analysis, and there were further discussions on *Panorama* and *Weekend World*. But it was three weeks after the retaking of South Georgia that pictures of the Union Jack being unfurled by the Royal Marines were shown for the first time.

Pictures of the stricken *Sheffield* taken on 7 May were finally shown in London on 28 May, two days *after* the screening of interviews with *Sheffield* survivors and her Captain, Sam Salt, which had been filmed within twenty-four hours of the ship being hit on 4 May. On-the-spot voice reports by the BBC's Brian Hanrahan and Robert Fox and ITN's Michael Nicholson gave detailed and graphic accounts, but much was left to the imagination of the listener, who could not possibly know of the real impact of an Exocet missile because they had never been fired in a war before. The daily scramble for news when so few facts were available led to front page stories like that in the *Sun* of 28 April, which, under the headline 'In We Go', reported troops moving in for battle three weeks *ahead* of the landing on 21 May. In fairness this story was topped by the Ministry of Defence news management of the actual San Carlos Bay landings. On the morning of Friday 21 May, when 3,000 troops were already ashore, all Britain's dailies carried stories based on the previous afternoon's Defence Ministry briefing that there would be no D-Day style invasion.

Scepticism at some of the television and newspaper coverage was reinforced by artists' impressions of what they thought was happening. At times the drawings and words used to describe Operation Corporate looked more like comic strip stories from *Dan Dare* and the *Eagle*. The *Sun* surpassed itself. In his book, *The Media, the Government and the Falklands Crisis*, Robert Harris analyses the *Sun*'s coverage in terms of a new video game called 'Obliterate', which the paper featured on 10 April. The game, in which the player is supposed to be the commander of a British submarine trying to torpedo Argentine ships, was almost a model for the paper's presentation of the war as real-life sport. In the *Sun*'s words, Britain threatened to 'shoot Argies out of the skies', while 'Navy helicopters blasted two gunboats to smithereens'. Harris comments: 'The jubilant "GOTCHA!" which greeted the sinking of the *Belgrano* was no aberration. It was the logical conclusion of the *Sun*'s coverage. It was the equivalent of ZAP! or POW! – or a headline which the *Sun* used later in the war – WALLOP!'

After the war, the scramble to be first with the 'untold' story of the South Atlantic Campaign led to a publishing boom in instant history books, war correspondents' diaries, television video films, glossy magazine series to be collected weekly and mounted in their special binders – a media event as brief as the war itself, now packaged in paperback to be shelved and forgotten. For those who are still coping with the aftermath of that war – the widows, the wives with husbands injured physically and mentally, the parents grieving for their sons and, in some cases, nursing their shattered bodies – the public memory is cruelly short.

Because their hunger for news had not been satisfied by inadequate early media coverage, families were unprepared for the realities of this war. Even after they had been told that their men had died or been injured, they could not imagine what it had really been like for them. They were doubly shocked when delayed pictures of the crippled *Sheffield* appeared on their television screens, and they also saw the brief burial in body bags of Lieutenant Colonel Herbert 'H' Jones and his men in a bleak battlefield, and the survivors of the blazing *Sir Galahad* stumbling ashore at Bluff Cove. For many bereaved families, even the details they pieced together from the returning troops who had been with their husbands and sons did not satisfy their quest for information. For those who chose to go on the Ministry of Defence organised visit to the Falklands a year later, it was as much a journey of discovery as to pay their respects – for some the journey confirmed their suspicion that no one would ever be able to answer their final question: 'How had it happened?'

It is little wonder that Lynda Gallagher's SAS husband, writing to her from the South Atlantic, told her not to believe

13

what she read in the newspapers. The Special Air Services had direct communication with their Hereford base, and no doubt those back home recounted some of the wilder speculation in the media about their colleagues' exploits in South Georgia. In fact it was Sergeant Major Lawrence Gallagher who raised the Union Jack after the British Antarctic Survey base at Grytviken was retaken, but, for publicity purposes and to preserve the anonymity of the SAS, the Royal Marines had been photographed around the flag pole instead.

The men's letters home, while revealing they were as much in the dark as their families were, tried to be reassuring and to concentrate on personal news. Lynda Gallagher had written to tell her husband that she was pregnant, just as she had thought the morning he left home. Maureen Emly had just two letters from Richard. One – when his ship the *Sheffield* was halfway to the Falklands – said the crew did not think it would come to anything, it was just a show of force. The second, dated 29 April, said: 'We are on action stations but everything will be all right.' Maureen still wonders if that is what he really believed, or if he was trying to comfort her. Caroline Hailwood poignantly summarises the change of mood in Christopher's letters home from the *Sir Galahad*: 'Towards the end Chris started writing romantic letters, the sort of love letters he had never ever written to me before when he was away. His writing deteriorated to a scrawl and he was obviously very tired.' Para Jason Burt's first letter home was a plea to his mum to send creams and medicated talcum powders to treat the Athlete's Foot he was suffering from after a ten-mile march across Ascension Island, the Paras first chance really to stretch their legs after weeks on the *Canberra*. Sergeant Ian McKay, one of two soldiers in the Parachute Regiment posthumously awarded the Victoria Cross, sent a postcard to his family in Rotherham saying he had been fishing off the stern of the *Canberra*; his letters tried to convince them it was just an exercise. Later, dug-in on the Falklands, he wrote of the frustrations of waiting for politicians in England to make up their minds about the battle order when the men just wanted to get it over with and go home.

In an attempt to correct speculative media stories and quash the rumours that spread through married quarters before they caused communal panic, some of the Forces welfare officers held briefing sessions and circulated news bulletins. The initiative was very much a hit-and-miss affair. Lynda Gallagher recalls that it was only after nineteen SAS men had died in a helicopter crash that weekly information sessions for the families were held at their Hereford base. Maureen Emly says there may have been briefings for the Royal Navy wives in married quarters in Portsmouth but nobody contacted her about them at her own home. When Sue Enefer in Plymouth phoned 45 Commando in Arbroath, Scotland, for news of her husband's whereabouts they did not have her name on the families list but later mailed her news letters of social events at the camp. Anita Flanagan and Dorothy Foulkes, whose husbands were on the *Altantic Conveyor*, got no news from Cunard, but Anita was compensated with information from her Royal Navy neighbours. Caroline Hailwood knew no families living locally whose men were on the *Sir Galahad* with her husband Christopher and told me that in retrospect she was glad for her social isolation, which she feels helped her keep up some semblance of normal life, which cushioned her from the collective anxieties in married quarters where neighbours and friends all had men in the task force. She did get a ship's news letter forwarded to the families of the *Sir Galahad*'s crew which was out of date by the time it reached them. She also received a circular about area coffee mornings for wives. She remembers: 'The Captain's wife phoned a couple of times to see if I was all right, and she came over to lunch one day, but even she didn't know what was happening.'

Marica McKay, whose twenty-nine-year-old husband, Ian, was a Para platoon sergeant, neatly summarised the common response of the military to families waiting at home for news of their men: 'In the Army there are no explanations just orders, and that rule applies to the families too. The Argentines had invaded, the men were sent to sort it out, and there was never any time to explain why.'

In Plymouth, a city which had more men in the task force than any other in Britain, there was one woman determined that their families would be given as much information as possible. Meg Baxter, the forty-one-year-old wife of Colonel Ian Baxter is both persuasive and disarming. Her incisive, sometimes abrasive manner is softened by her very feminine dress and ash blonde hair; sometimes she sounds a bit like the private girls' school headmistress she once was but insists she has kept the down-to-earth values of her working class childhood. Meg Baxter has seen as much of military life as any senior officer's wife; in twenty-two years of marriage she has moved house seventeen times because of her husband's work. She is proud of his profession, and especially of him; she willingly fulfils the duties expected of a Commanding Officer's wife, is her three daughters' best friend and works as a freelance broadcaster and journalist.

She knew that coordinating information from the three Services and communicating with task force families was going to be a major problem: 'Especially for the Royal Navy who had not dealt with a war for some time.' Meg had written a column for an Army newspaper when stationed in Germany. She approached the local evening paper with some of her cuttings and a suggestion she write a regular article on what was happening to the task force, where families could get more information and when social events and briefing sessions were being held; 'The sort of information the national press would not be interested in but you could put in a local paper. The Falklands really only touched certain communities like Plymouth. But here it was not just a question of keeping the immediate next-of-kin informed – sisters, brothers, aunts and grannies wanted to know what was going on. I don't know how the Services would have coped with all their inquiries if we had not anticipated a lot of their questions in my column.' The paper was enthusiastic, so were the local Armed Forces public relations and welfare officers. Meg Baxter set up an office in her home at Crown Hill Fort, which quickly became a twenty-four hour clearing house for all three Services. She was aware that in some quarters there was a feeling that it was not the done thing for a Colonel's wife to be involved in that side of the men's work, but it was acceptable given the exceptional circumstances.

This was nothing like the Second World War, where the whole nation was threatened by an enemy just miles across the English Channel. The Falklands War fully involved only certain communities: the military garrison towns of Aldershot; the market town of Hereford, the home base of the SAS; the naval dockyards of Portsmouth and Plymouth. It was

16

particularly traumatic for those families whose men were in the Royal Navy and up to then had been thankful that they had never had to worry about their sons and husbands going to Northern Ireland.

Mrs Patricia Stockwell's Petty Officer son, Geoffrey, was a marine engineering artificer officer on HMS *Coventry*, the sister ship of the *Sheffield*, which was also despatched to the South Atlantic instead of returning home after the NATO exercise Springtrain. She and her husband, Leslie, had worked in the Admiralty during the Second World War and it was incomprehensible to them that – after thirty-seven years of peace – their only son was going to war in a Service he had joined because he loved the sea, sport and travel.

The social isolation of families living some distance from the Service communities accentuated feelings of unreality about what was happening. Rosemary Anslow, whose twenty-year-old son, Adrian, was a Fleet Air Arm mechanic on the *Atlantic Conveyor*, sometimes felt like running up to people in the streets of Wolverhampton where she lived and shaking them: 'I could not understand just why everyday life was carrying on around me when my son was at war.'

But Britain never was at war. Throughout the Falklands conflict, war was never ever officially declared by either side. There was no nationally based *civil* response to the particular needs of the task force families, initially for news of their men, and later to handle bereavement and injury. The consequences of the war were left to the Armed Forces. The Forces are a private world based on a rigid social and command structure geared to group cohesion. Uniforms, rank, rule books, regimental customs enhance their separate values – in a society in which many women can no longer be expected to see themselves in the traditional roles expected of them by an all-male military hierarchy. The role of wives in the Armed Forces, however, is still a social one, a concept which does not allow for individuality or personal needs. In times of conflict, like that in the South Atlantic, women are expected to cope, as they always have done on the home front, with the domestic aftermath of battle – death and injury. But in 1982 the Armed Forces found themselves with a non-conscript generation of Service families; wives and mothers of

17

Servicemen who were no longer prepared quietly or meekly 'to mop-up'. Marica McKay has commented that in the Army there are no explanations, just orders, and that rule applies to families too. It is a social attitude as outdated as the secrecy of the Armed Forces.

The Falklands War revealed that chauvinism and secrecy – primarily through the raised voices of women.

CHAPTER TWO:

How they gave 'the Bad News'

'Governments should go on talking for as long as possible before using guns.' Marica McKay, widow of Sergeant Ian McKay, VC.

The worst weeks for Maureen Emly had been after Richard's homeward-bound ship, the *Sheffield*, had been re-routed to the South Atlantic and no one seemed to know what was going to happen next. There had been few clues in the shuttle diplomacy and media speculation, as the task force neared the Falklands. Any optimism that the crisis would be over by the time Rear Admiral Sandy Woodward's armada reached Ascension Island was at odds with the battle drills of the Scots and Welsh Guards and Gurkhas in the Brecon Beacons, as they prepared to leave on the requisitioned Cunard liner *QE2*. Maureen scoured the newspapers and swiched from the radio to television in search of news but the facts from the various reports were contradictory and she was left on edge. 'Just not knowing anything, it was sheer hell.' The Argentines had invaded the Falklands on 2 April and the only undisputed development was the retaking of South Georgia on 25 April.

For Maureen Emly, after a month in the dark, the news of the *General Belgrano* came almost as a relief. The British submarine *Conqueror* sank the Argentine cruiser with the loss of 368 lives on 2 May outside the total exclusion zone. At last Maureen knew for a fact that this was war; and, like many of the wives of the *Sheffield*'s crew, her apprehension became a premonition. She was convinced that something was about to happen to her husband's ship because, she reasoned, there had to be a reprisal for the *Belgrano*, and the *Sheffield*, being the first to leave, would be the first to arrive and, therefore, the first in the firing line.

And, indeed, the *Sheffield*, a Type 42 destroyer with 270 men on board, was on picket duty about twenty miles ahead of the main task force when it was hit by an Exocet missile amidships just above the water-line shortly after 2 pm on 4 May. After four-and-a-half hours spent trying to save the blistering, smoke-filled destroyer her Captain, Sam Salt, gave the order to 'Abandon ship'.

Maureen heard that the ship had been hit in the same way as she had heard of its departure for the South Atlantic – on the radio. She and her sister Pat and their neighbours sat up all night dialling every half hour the Portsmouth dockyard telephone numbers broadcast on the radio and television for the next of kin, but the lines were continuously engaged. When they finally got through at 7.45 am they were told Richard Emly had survived.

Three hours later, when Maureen was in the bath, a Royal Navy chaplain came to the house and she told her sister to send him away because she would not listen to him. The chaplain called again that afternoon to confirm that Richard Emly, aged thirty-six, later to be named in despatches for his bravery, was missing presumed dead. There were no apologies or explanations for the earlier mistake. Maureen still wonders how they got it so cruelly wrong: it was an unusual name and no one on the ship was called anything similar. For a week she lay curled up in the corner of their bed, the news of her husband's death magnified by the unreality of how it had happened: 'It is impossible to describe the feeling when a healthy young man is killed in such a totally unexpected way. The circumstances were shocking. It is not the same as an illness or an accident. To die in a war seemed unbelievable, he was in the Royal Navy.' Had Richard been in the Army, Maureen felt, there would always have been the risk of active service in Northern Ireland, where 722 members of the Security Forces have been killed since 1969.

The news of the *Sheffield* stunned Britain. The bragging tones of a Rear-Admiral's 'walk-over' were as inappropriate now as the strident self-confidence of a Prime Minister who, at the outset of the war, had insisted, 'Defeat? The possibility does not exist.' Behind the drawn curtains of twenty homes in Britain defeat did exist, in the loss of twenty men from HMS *Sheffield*.

Anita Flanagan and her neighbours in their Royal Navy married headquarters in Rainham were hunched around a television set watching the BBC's *Nine O'Clock News*, when the political editor, John Cole, was interrupted in his report of that day's events in the House of Commons and the programme's cameras switched live to the Ministry of Defence and its official Falklands War spokesman, Ian McDonald. Months later Anita could recite almost the exact words of that dramatic bulletin delivered in McDonald's measured monotone: 'In the course of its duties the HMS *Sheffield* was attacked and hit this afternoon by an Argentine missile. The ship caught fire and when there was no longer any hope of saving her the ship's company abandoned ship. All who abandoned her were picked up but there have been a number of casualties and the next of kin will be informed as soon as the details are received.' There had been no hint that such a devastating item was about to be broadcast into the sitting rooms of the task force families, no attempt to cushion the impact. Ian McDonald's sudden materialisation on millions of TV screens was the first the public knew of the stricken *Sheffield*. Even the House of Commons had to demand a statement from the Defence Secretary, John Nott. At 11 pm that night he revealed the shocked confusion inside his own ministry when, in the middle of his speech, he revised the estimate of the number of crew missing from twelve to thirty after a note was passed to him. The final casualty list was twenty dead and twenty-four injured.

Anita and her friends had sought each other out almost every evening after their husbands had left for the Falklands, to watch and listen together in their homes for news of their men. They received McDonald's statement in silence, which seconds later erupted in anger. Twenty-four hours earlier Anita had greeted the sinking of the *Belgrano* with cheers of: 'Serve them right, they should not have started it in the first place.' Now it was: 'How dare they do that to one of ours?' In retrospect, she realises it was an irrational, jingoistic response, but she had assumed that – because the *General Belgrano* had been sunk by the submarine *Conqueror* outside the exclusion zone – none of the task force ships was close enough to the Falklands for such a swift reprisal. It had been a month since the first British ships left for the South Atlantic and there had been no indication of their whereabouts until an airborne Exocet missile targeted the *Sheffield* and revealed that the task force was now in range of the Argentine air force. Although none of Anita's neighbours had men on the ship, after weeks of worry the *Sheffield* was the reality of what might happen to them.

As she listened to the reports of the sinking of the *Belgrano*, Caroline Hailwood was completely fatalistic about her husband Chris, one of the Royal Fleet Auxiliary crew on the landing ship *Sir Galahad*. From the moment when she and her baby son had left Chris at Plymouth's Devonport dockyard on 5 April, shadowed by the paraphernalia of war, she had been convinced that she would not see him again. And the day the ship left Plymouth, Chris himself had sought out the Captain's wife and had asked her to take care of his wife and son.

Caroline now rationalises her fatalism in terms of mentally preparing herself for the worst, because she had found the whole situation so incomprehensible that she had believed anything could happen. With Chris on his way to the South Atlantic and the Easter holidays and her maternity leave ended, she concentrated on returning to her teaching job at a nearby school in Farnborough. She arranged a routine with a local child minder for her son Jim, so he did not miss his father too much or her absence during the day when she was working. Her spare time was spent organising the building work on the house they had planned to move into by June. At school, her colleagues tried to convince her that the *Sir Galahad*, a supply ship with no air defence system, would not go anywhere near the Falklands and would stay out of range of the fighting. Caroline knew otherwise; she had witnessed the loading of equipment and the bedding down of troops, and guessed the ship would ferry both right into the islands.

Caroline told me how she busied herself packing up the flat for the move to their new home and found among her husband's souvenirs from earlier trips overseas postcards, stamps and coins from the Falklands which he had visited on a British patrol ship before they had met. He had loved the bleak solitude of the islands with their teeming wildlife; and he had managed to joke before saying goodbye that the whole exercise was a charade, they were just a Save the Penguin Brigade. As she packed, Caroline moved around the flat with the radio switched on, anxious not to miss any news. The loss of the *Sheffield* confirmed her belief that her husband would not return.

The *Sheffield*'s fate really shook Dorothy Foulkes, whose Petty Officer husband Frank was the chief mechanic on Cunard's container ship the *Atlantic Conveyor*. Like Anita Flanagan, whose Royal Navy husband Edmund had been posted to the *Atlantic Conveyor*, she had believed that the sinking of the *Belgrano* would show the aggressors what Britain was made of and they would scuttle home without a fight. Once the *Sheffield* was hit, Dorothy knew there was no going back and that Margaret Thatcher had a battle royal on her hands.

Marica McKay, whose husband Ian was with the 3rd Battalion Parachute Regiment on the *Canberra*, was equally convinced that, given the nationality of General Leopold Galtieri and the personality of the British Prime Minister, it would be a bitterly fought campaign. 'Galtieri is a Latin American and it was a matter of personal as well as national pride to continue regardless of the circumstances. From the start Margaret Thatcher talked and behaved like Queen Victoria, so what could you expect of a woman who believed she ruled the world? Governments should go on talking for as long as possible before using guns but after the *Belgrano* there was no going back.'

In Surrey, the Pirbright barracks and modern housing estate of the married quarters of the 1st Battalion of the Welsh Guards was a community left almost devoid of men. Some of the wives with babies and toddlers had gone home to stay with their families, in the belief their husbands would not return until November when they would be relieved from garrison duty on the reoccupied Falkland Islands. A few of the soldiers' wives with children at local schools and jobs of their own moved in with neighbours to keep each other company and share the child-minding and household bills.

Jane Keoghane was five months pregnant with her first child. Her husband Kevin, a Lance Sergeant, had talked the previous Christmas of leaving the regiment for the police force because at thirty he felt his promotion was slower than expected. It was a decision that would have delighted Jane, but she also knew that he would probably regret it as the Army was his life. He had been brought up to be a soldier by his father, who had retired from the Welsh Guards as a company sergeant major.

Jane's brother Bobby had served time with the regiment. Bobby had met and married a local girl, Renate, while on a posting in Germany, before he had returned to live in the family's home town of Newport when he left the Army. Jane had not envied her sister-in-law's lifestyle as a soldier's wife, moving around, living in married quarters, coping alone with two small children during long separations when Bobby was abroad or in Northern Ireland; Jane had decided she would never marry someone from the Armed Forces. She was working at Westminster Hospital, London, as a nursing sister with her own flat and a good social life when she dropped in on Bobby and his wife, who were then stationed at Caterham. It was a Saturday and she was invited that night by one of Bobby's fellow soldiers to go to the Guards' June ball, where she met Kevin Keoghane. She still smiles at how easily she was won over to the idea of being a soldier's wife. 'My brother Bobby was in the Guards and I thought I knew what to expect, but I did not really know what I was letting myself in for when I married Kevin. His loyalty to the regiment was total. He drank, ate and slept the Welsh Guards. It was his career and he took great pride in what he did, his drill was immaculate and he knew his mortars back to front.' It is not surprising the regiment were reluctant to lose him and when one of the officers heard he was thinking of leaving he was promised he would soon get his sash as a full sergeant.

Jane and Kevin had been married six years, having spent the first three in Berlin, where Jane continued her career by running a medical centre for the Green Howards and later the 2nd Battalion Royal Anglians. A few months after their return to England Kevin did a seven-month tour of Northern

Ireland, a separation Jane used to complete a year's diploma course at Surrey University in community nursing which qualified her for a job with the North West Surrey health authority. She enjoyed the variety and demands of her work but was really looking forward to giving it a rest to spend all her time with their much-wanted baby and creating a home of their own. Whatever Kevin decided to do about his Army career, with a baby on the way they both wanted roots and a family home.

Jane Keoghane's professional awareness was to make her personal experience of how the Army handled the consequences of the Falklands War that much more difficult to come to terms with. Apart from her understanding of nursing, there were the expectations of how a traditional, family-based regiment like the Welsh Guards would behave towards the victims of a war. Guardsmen's wives, such as Jane Keoghane, believed that if anything happened to their men the regiment would look after them. The military encouraged the concept of the family because it fostered the feeling of brotherhood among serving soldiers and reinforced group cohesion and regimental loyalty. But in practice the behaviour expected of a caring family is not part of its ethos. Although the military prides itself on being a self-sufficient society with its own social, welfare, medical and housing schemes, the Falklands War exposed its weakness in handling the inevitable consequences of all wars – death and injury. Its stubborn inability to acknowledge that it could not cope with a post-conscript generation of Servicemen and their families only made things worse. When people complained, they were made to feel that they were 'stepping out of line', that any criticism was 'letting down' the regiment, and it was not the 'done thing' publicly to question 'Why?'

The government should never have left the Services to deal alone with the impact of the war on task force families. Their approach was out of date to a generation who had grown up in the Welfare State and believed it their right to be treated compassionately when in need. The support and comfort given to some families by individuals in the Armed Forces – particularly by returning officers who had fought alongside their men – was in keeping with the traditions of paternalism inherent in the rank structure. These were caring, senior people, personally aware of social change. But, overall, the Armed Forces' domestic procedures were totally inadequate for responding to the aftermath of a military conflict in the Eighties on the scale of Operation Corporate. The government should have made it their business to oversee, or at least coordinate, the care of the bereaved and injured.

The treatment of these families depended very much on which Service or regiment their men belonged to, and where they lived. The confusion and distress of some of the parents of the 121 single men who were killed was often made worse by their social isolation from the unfamiliar world of their sons' Service lives. It was the same sense of alienation as that felt by Dorothy Foulkes, who had never expected her merchant seaman husband Frank, a non-combatant, to be involved in a war.

Even the way the news of casualties was given to the families varied from Service to Service. The Royal Air Force were fortunate in having only one casualty throughout the Falklands War, the Army had well-tested procedures because of their role in Northern Ireland, but the Royal Navy had not handled such a situation since the Second World War. They set up their own in-house schemes. In theory, a naval officer and chaplain would be despatched to families to break the news of casualties. At the naval dockyards of Chatham, Plymouth, Portsmouth and Faslane, banks of emergency telephones were manned twenty-four hours to answer inquiries and officers' wives were detailed to organise telephone chains linking families whose men were on the same ship. In practice, the systems were often pre-empted by unexpected announcements, like Ian McDonald's broadcast on the *Sheffield* disaster, or John Nott's reports in which no accurate figures of casualties or even the names of ships were given. On such occasions, the shambles in coordinating information caused unnecessary heartache to hundreds of task force families.

News of the *Sheffield* was traumatic for families of troops en route to the Falklands who, for security reasons, were not supposed to reveal in their letters which ship they were on. For the first time in her married life, Lynda Gallagher was worried about where her SAS husband Lawrence might be.

She called a friend, the regimental sergeant major's wife, to see if she knew which ship the men were on. She did not, but Lawrence had been right: 'This was the Real Thing.'

Lynda just hoped Lawrence was safe on land, for once ashore with a gun in his hand she believed him invincible. By the middle of May he had certainly been on land at least twice, the first time in South Georgia, and again on 14 May when the SAS raided the airstrip at Pebble Island north of West Falkland and blew up eleven Argentine aircraft. That Spring, Lynda a tall, extrovert blonde, was plump with the pleasure of a healthy pregnancy. She spent her days doing what she enjoyed most when Lawrence was away, knitting, sewing, visiting her parents and sister who lived nearby, and keeping up with her energetic daughters, five-year-old Kirsty and Dawn-Marie, aged two. Lawrence Gallagher adored his children but his wife knew that – much as he liked being at home with them all – after a few months back at the SAS Hereford base he was ready to go away again. He had been in his late twenties when they had met and married, and she knew there was no chance of changing him or his dedication to the Army. 'He would not have been the man I married if he had not become restless to get back to doing the work he was so good at, and I would not have wanted him any other way.'

Lynda, whose Scots parents had moved to Hereford when she was a child, had quickly adapted to unscheduled separations. The well-heeled, country market town, with its historic cathedral, is very different from Army garrison towns like Aldershot, or the Royal Navy ports of Portsmouth and Chatham, where barracks and Service quarters are often separate from other residential areas. In London, soldiers and their families live in blocks of flats behind spotlit walls, where (because of threats of terrorist attacks) armed guards stand at all entrances and casual visitors are discouraged. Hereford is the permanent home-base of the Special Air Services and their role in the Armed Forces is as highly mobile, covert trouble-shooters. Their families rarely, if ever, move around with them, even on short-term postings abroad. Lynda and Lawrence, like the majority of Hereford-based Army couples, never lived in married quarters. To the other residents on the street where they bought their home, they were just another family where the husband was 'something to do with the

Army'. Many of Lawrence's fellow soldiers had married local girls and the Gallaghers had as many civilian as Army friends, and were more likely to spend an evening in a town pub than at the social club on the camp or at the sergeants' mess.

For Lynda and other SAS wives, social integration in a civilian community, where many of their own families lived, cushioned them against the isolation felt by many Service wives living in married quarters when their husbands were away. Loneliness and adapting to new people and neighbourhoods was a problem for many young, housebound wives who had moved from posting to posting with their husbands, particularly when the husband was sent to Northern Ireland soon after the family had moved to a new town. It is not surprising that some of the Welsh Guards' young wives at Pirbright went home to mums when their husbands left for the Falklands, or that some wives reached the stage when they wanted to stay put in their own homes – their children's schooling uninterrupted and their own careers continued – while their husbands move to yet another temporary posting.

Unlike the Royal Marines, and in particular the Parachute Regiment, whose regular media appearances make them the most competitive branch of the Armed Services for new recruits, the SAS shun publicity as the nature of their work does not permit too much public scrutiny. They disliked the saturation coverage of their successful retaking of the Iranian Embassy in Princes Gate, London, in May 1980 when their dramatic eleven-minute assault was carried out in front of the world's press, including live television transmission. They disapproved even more of the glamorised, largely inaccurate newspaper and magazine series, books and a film that cashed in on the incident. But the stories confirmed what the people of Hereford had known for some time – that some extraordinary and brave men lived in their town – and in the Summer of 1982 everyone responded to the death of nineteen SAS soldiers in the South Atlantic as though they were their own family.

It was one of Lawrence's fellow soldiers and his wife who came to tell Lynda on Friday 21 May that, two days before, her husband and eighteen other SAS soldiers had drowned when their Sea King helicopter crashed into the sea. For the first few days she thought the helicopter, which had been about to land on the assault ship *Intrepid*, had been tipped into the sea as a wave lifted the boat deck. Then she heard how the Sea King had struck an albatross which embedded itself in the engine, cutting out the power and plunging the helicopter into the water. The irony of her husband's death still makes Lynda angry; she feels it would have been easier to accept if he had died with a gun in his hand, rather than a helpless victim in a freak accident. She told me: 'Later one of his colleagues came to see me and said they had been in so many dangerous situations together he believed Lawrence was infallible to bullets, when his time came it had to be another way.' Lynda remembers how the whole town seemed to go into a state of shock; it was the biggest single loss the SAS had had since it was formed as a regiment in 1942. This was a family affair; there was communal grief and a protective closing of ranks around the bereaved families against inquisitive outsiders and the press. The civic response to a fund for the fifteen SAS widows rapidly raised £63,000.

The war was over for Lynda Gallagher. She did not bother with the news any more. She just concentrated on staying well enough not to miscarry the baby, although it was not until ten long days after her husband had died that she received a letter from him saying 'how wonderful' had been the news that she was pregnant. In the following months, she lost one-and-a-half stones and tried to keep from the doctor she was smoking forty cigarettes a day. Lynda now believes it was only because she was so healthy at the beginning of her pregnancy that she did not lose the 6lb 9oz baby girl born in a hurry in her kitchen seven months later.

On the morning of 21 May, the British press carried stories (based on a Ministry of Defence briefing the day before) that no D-Day style landing would take place in the Falklands, when in fact 3,000 troops were already ashore at San Carlos. That evening at her home in the Cornish village of Landrake, June Evans heard on a television news bulletin that two small helicopters had been shot down during the San Carlos landings. There were no details of casualties but she was convinced one of them was her husband, Sergeant Andy Evans of 3 Commando Brigade.

She describes the seven weeks after he left home as days of

29

'sheer terror', her stomach churning every time she heard the theme music for the ITN *News at Ten*. The week before the troops embarked at San Carlos she had tried to imagine where they might go ashore, as she knew from Andy's work in Northern Ireland that his Gazelle helicopter did reconnaissance work, manoeuvring behind buildings and trees to avoid potential attack. She also knew from everything she had read and seen about the Falklands that there were few buildings, and fewer trees on the islands, and for days the words 'No trees' had occupied her thoughts, making it difficult to concentrate on her work as a clerical officer at Devonport dockyard, or to be patient with her children, eleven-year-old Mark and Samantha, aged eight.

The children had also heard the television news and gone quietly to bed, leaving June so wide awake at two in the morning that she took a sleeping tablet. She was still awake when she heard the knock at her front door at 4 am and opened it to a neighbour, Royal Marine Captain Brian Warriner and his wife. She knew exactly what he meant when he said: 'June, it's Andy.' It was almost a relief, and she invited them in for coffee. The news spread quickly through the tiny village and it seemed everyone came to pay their respects. 'It must have looked a bit like a scene from a Greek tragedy, a room full of women who just came and sat with me for hours until my relatives arrived. Everyone was incredibly kind, they just couldn't do enough for us, the only surprise was that I had expected the vicar to break the news rather than Captain Warriner. I was lucky living in a small community where Andy was well known and liked by everybody.'

The Evans family originated from Lancashire and June had moved house seven times to different postings with her husband until two years previously, when they had decided that – whatever Andy's future with the Royal Marines – they would make their home and bring up their children in Cornwall, which they both loved. Their first summer at their own home in Landrake, Andy had landed his helicopter in the school playing fields opposite their house during the village carnival – June can still remember the pride on her son Mark's face as his father demonstrated the controls to the village children. Andy belonged to the village badminton club and was a regular at the nearby Buller's Arms, where customers left £200 for his family in his personal beer mug placed by the landlord on the corner of the bar. The parish church held a packed memorial service and later, with none of the bitterness and controversy that marked other public commemorations to the Falklands dead, quietly added Andy Evans' name to the village memorial for men from Landrake killed in the First and Second World Wars.

It was not until Andy's unit returned to Plymouth in July that June was given the full details of her husband's death by his co-pilot, whose account of Andy's valour earned him a posthumous mention in despatches for distinguished service.

June Evans was not the only one in the Plymouth area that night who waited anxiously for a knock on her door after hearing the television news. John Nott's statement to the House of Commons on the San Carlos landings included the item that five British war ships were reported hit by Argentine aircraft, but the report did not name them. Staff answering the local Royal Navy's emergency telephones logged 5,000 calls in the next twenty-four hours, many of them unnecessary as the callers' relatives were not on the ships that had been hit. Two of those calls were made by Christina Heyes, whose able seaman husband Stephen, twenty-one, was on the frigate HMS *Ardent*.

Christina was part of a telephone chain, but she was anxious that somebody might have tried to call her while she was out at work as a barmaid. When she returned home, she dialled the emergency number at HMS *Drake*. She was reassured that the casualties did not include the *Ardent* and she was given the same information when she called the following morning before leaving for work. At midday one of her customers walked in and said he had just heard that the Argentines had sunk the *Ardent*. Three hours later a Royal Navy chaplain and officer called at the home the Heyes couple had moved into forty-eight hours before Stephen left for the Falklands, and just days after their first wedding anniversary. They told Christina that her husband was missing, presumed dead.

A group of Plymouth-based wives of other *Ardent* crewmen were in the middle of taping video messages for their husbands, when someone burst in with the news that twenty-two crewmen had been killed.

On occasions like these the Ministry of Defence seems to have paid little attention to the Armed Forces procedures for informing the next of kin *before* releasing news items or House of Commons statements. The following week when the naval commanders at Fleet Headquarters Northwood decided, in the interests of security, to stop John Nott from naming the *Sheffield*'s sister ship, the *Coventry* – when it was hit by an Exocet missile, capsized and sunk within twenty minutes – thousands of task force families were left on a knife's edge waiting eighteen hours for the ship to be identified.

At their home in Herne Bay, Pat and Leslie Stockwell waited almost two days for news of their bachelor son, Geoffrey, a Royal Navy Petty Officer who celebrated his twenty-fifth birthday on board the *Coventry* in the South Atlantic. On Tuesday 25 May, Pat Stockwell returned from an evening with the local Red Cross and sat down, still wearing her coat, to watch the ITN *News at Ten*, in which John Nott announced they had received 'bad news' and continued: 'One of our ships has been badly damaged and she is in difficulties. I can't give any further details at the moment – the news is still coming in about her. Clearly from what we know at the moment it is bad news and I should say that straightaway.' Pat and her husband sat up all night phoning the Royal Navy's emergency numbers, desperate to know the name of the ship. On Wednesday morning Leslie, a retired civil servant and former Sheriff of Canterbury, phoned the Royal Navy barracks at Portsmouth and was told it was the *Coventry*, but they had no details. That afternoon in the House of Commons, John Nott named the ship and said the next of kin had been informed. The Stockwells continued to telephone the emergency numbers and were assured their son's name was not on any lists that had been received.

On Thursday morning Leslie, who was a Conservative councillor, called his MP, David Crouch, at the House of Commons. Crouch's secretary spoke to John Nott's office and told the Stockwells to expect to hear something by midday. It was then the Royal Navy padre came from Chatham to say Geoffrey was missing. While he was still there, a family friend phoned for news and Leslie told her his son was missing, believed killed; the padre leapt from his chair and said they knew only that he was missing. It was not until Saturday morning the family were told Geoffrey had to be presumed dead. His mother says: 'Those two days from Tuesday evening to Thursday lunch-time were the most unbearable days of my life.'

Pat Stockwell had been twenty-one at the beginning of the Second World War and had worked throughout in the Admiralty in London. She says her generation learned to live without news of their relatives and friends in the Services; she remembers a school friend's fiancé was taken prisoner by the Japanese and there was no means of knowing what happened to him for years. Pat, who married in her late thirties, was almost forty when she had her son Geoffrey, followed fifteen months later by her daughter Ruth. 'Our children were a precious bonus. I never thought after what we had lived through in the Second World War, and then all those years of peace, that my son would die like that.'

The young marine engineering artificer had been an exceptional student and sportsman. He had been captain of the Royal Navy's under-21 hockey team and played for their senior side and combined Services' team. His sports equipment was lost with the ship, but a Naval officer team-mate bought a new track suit and, complete with a Combined Services badge, personally presented it to his parents. The Chatham-based Royal Navy families' officer, and the padre, kept in touch with the family for some time after the loss of their son to see if they could help in any way.

Anita Flanagan also heard John Nott's announcement on Tuesday evening while watching television at her neighbour's house. She did not, as on previous occasions, call the Royal Navy's emergency numbers to ask about the *Atlantic Conveyor*. Instead she went home and, for the first time in seventeen nights, slept without the recurrent dream of swimming in the sea towards her husband Edmund, although she cannot swim. She recalled the dream for me as though looking at a much-thumbed photograph. To the right of her, lit up by fire, was the *Atlantic Conveyor* with a gaping hole in her side. Edmund, still wearing his spectacles and dressed in a navy wool pullover, but minus his peaked cap, faced her, treading water.

Anita could hear the sound of the sea. As she swam towards him he disappeared and she awoke.

At 8 am, the morning after that dreamless night, while getting her children Cassandra and Tarquin ready for school, there was a knock on the door and a young lieutenant asked if he could come in. Anita knew why he had come and held the door ajar, insisting he stay where he was and talk to her. She thought if she did not let him in he could not tell her and it would not have happened. He refused to say any more until eventually she took him into the sitting room. When he told her, she hit him. She says: 'He was as white as a sheet, a stranger, on his own, too young to have known what a war was, never mind tell somebody what they had sent him to tell me. It was not his fault, it really was not handled very well, but I later sent a letter apologising for my behaviour.' Cassandra came into the kitchen and asked her mother to help her put up her long hair so she could go to school. Anita remembers taking her by the hand and going next door to her neighbour and saying: 'You will have to do my daughter's hair as Edmund has been killed.' The house was soon packed with people. Anita felt quite calm between making pots of tea and telephone calls, until she was taken aside by a Royal Navy chaplain, who suggested they go into the quiet of her garden to pray. 'At that point I got very angry and the doctor came and gave me some pills to calm down.'

The neighbours could not do enough for the Flanagan family, but after Edmund died the women no longer sat together in the evenings watching television for news of their husbands' ships.

John Nott announced the loss of Edmund Flanagan's ship, the *Atlantic Conveyor*, when he named the *Coventry* in the House of Commons on Wednesday 26 May; strategically, because of its cargo, it was the most damaging loss of the whole of the campaign. Edmund was one of the Royal Navy crew posted to the requisitioned Cunard container ship which was hit by an Exocet soon after the missile attack that sank the *Coventry*. The bomb exploded and fire rapidly spread through the ship, destroying her cargo, which included three giant troop carrier Chinook helicopters and enough tents for 4,000 soldiers, both earmarked for the task force advance on Port Stanley. Anita had been relieved when her husband joined a merchant vessel rather than a troopship or destroyer. It had no defence system and she believed it would distribute supplies to the task force from outside the combat zone. But the ship was fully operational within the total exclusion zone when it was hit.

Two days after he died, Anita received a letter from her husband written on 16 May saying he did not know what would happen if they were attacked as they were totally dependent on air cover. In addition to the helicopters, the *Atlantic Conveyor* had taken the RAF's reinforcement Harriers to the South Atlantic and once they were transferred to the aircraft carriers *Invincible* and *Hermes*, her empty deck space was used as an occasional parking lot for other aircraft operating in the area. The ship was on her way to the San Carlos beach-head to unload the rest of her supplies when she was bombed. At first it was thought only four crewmen were killed but the revised casualty list was twelve, including the Cunard Captain 'Birdseye', Ian North, and his chief mechanic, Petty Officer Frank Foulkes.

In the weeks her husband Frank had been at sea as a volunteer crewman on his requisitioned ship, Dorothy had felt strangely detached from the news of the war. She knew no families who had men in the task force, other than the ship's Cunard crew, and none of them lived nearby. Dorothy was familiar with her husband being away for nine weeks at a time on the trans-Atlantic cargo runs. 'I just didn't think that what was on the television had anything to do with him. He was in the Merchant Navy, and all the news was about the Royal Navy and the soldiers.' No one from Cunard's head office in London or the ship's home port of Liverpool had contacted her after Frank's departure. Technically, as a volunteer civilian in a military engagement, Petty Officer Foulkes was under orders from the task force fleet command at Northwood, and the Royal Navy's Captain Michael Layard had been seconded to the *Atlantic Conveyor* to work with Cunard's Captain North, but Dorothy received no news of the ship from the Navy either.

Dorothy had spent the morning of 26 May at the dentist with her two youngest daughters, Victoria and Charlotte, and as they stepped from their taxi a man got out of a car parked outside their drive and walked towards them. Dorothy spotted the blue seaman's badge in the lapel of his lounge suit as he introduced himself as Captain Clayton, the northern director for the Missions to Seamen from Manchester, and asked if they could go into the house. 'He said he was very sorry, they had some bad news, the worst.' She gave him the telephone numbers of her two grown-up children, but her daughter Angela had already heard through the Army Signal Corps, and rang her mother while Captain Clayton was at the house to say she and her husband were coming home on the overnight boat from Germany. Dorothy's son David's warrant officer at RAF Brize Norton sent him straight home in a chauffeur-driven car, and Dorothy remembers her surprise at seeing him in his uniform for the first time since his passing-out parade.

That afternoon an office administrator from the Cunard headquarters in Liverpool came to see the Foulkes family and Dorothy asked her to find out anything she could about how her husband had died. 'I just did not believe it had happened, I wanted to know all the details.' The Cunard offices in Liverpool and London insisted they had no details of individual casualties, but two weeks after Frank Foulkes died his widow opened her local paper, the *Evening Gazette*, and read the headline on page nine, 'Ship's surgeon relives missile attack horror'. It was a personal account by Surgeon Lieutenant Gordon Brooks, whose parents lived in Blackpool, of his last two hours on board the blazing *Atlantic Conveyor*. In the third paragraph he paid tribute to another local man, Frank Foulkes: 'One of the first people who went down below in a fire suit to try and rescue those trapped. He came back without having any success but he was extremely brave. He was in a damage patrol team whose job it was to do this thing'. What followed was a chilling and graphic account of the death throes of the crippled ship, including the screams of crew trapped by fire below decks, how the doctor tried to get to a life raft to lower an injured man but was beaten back by the smoke, how they all abandoned the ship and were eventually picked up by crew from the frigate HMS *Alacrity*. The survivors were later transferred to a cargo ship which took them to Ascension Island and a flight home to Brize Norton.

It was the first detailed information Dorothy had seen on the fate of her husband's ship and unexpectedly to read such a report, one that actually mentioned her husband's name, when Cunard had said they knew nothing, angered and distressed her. In her confused state she was convinced the badly-injured crewman the ship's doctor had tried to get into a life raft was Frank, and she rang the newspaper asking for Gordon Brooks' telephone number. The reporter told her it was not their practice to give telephone numbers to the public but as she was Frank Foulkes' widow they would make an exception. As Frank's widow, Dorothy wondered why they had not made an exception to contact her about the story before it was published. When she talked to Gordon Brooks at his Gosport home he, too, was upset at her distress but able to reassure her that Frank was not the injured man he had unsuccessfully tried to help. He told her he had later identified Frank's body when it was picked up by crewmen from *Alacrity* and that Frank had drowned, untouched by the fire. Afterwards he sent her a photograph of Frank he had taken on their voyage to the Falklands.

When Dorothy heard that Cunard had held an inquest on the *Atlantic Conveyor* she again rang for information and was told there was nothing further to add. They did send her a piece of paper, a photostat copy of a shipping chart of the waters around the Falklands, on which they had marked a cross and typed above it 'position of the burial at sea of Mr Frank Foulkes at 15.50 GMT 26 May 1982'. Brandishing the much-examined document, she told me: 'That was all the "detail" I ever got from Cunard.'

The first casualties of the war were buried at sea. But once the task force had established itself on the San Carlos beach-head then, true to the traditions of the British Army, the men were laid to rest on the battlefield. When Sue Enefer learned of the death of her Royal Marine husband, Sergeant Roger Enefer of 45 Commando, who was killed with three other soldiers from his company on 27 May in an attack on their trenches, she told the Marines that she wanted him brought back for burial, even if she had to pay for it herself.

On the Friday morning when a Royal Marine Captain and his wife came from the Plymouth barracks to tell her about Roger, she would not at first believe it. After the San Carlos landing the week before, Colonel's wife Meg Baxter, in her local evening paper column had advised Plymouth-based task force families not to listen to blow-by-blow accounts on the radio and television. But Sue had become so dependent on the radio and TV, as the only source of news, that she had set her radio alarm for the 7 am news headlines. As there was nothing in that morning's bulletin about casualties, she briefly clung to the belief that her husband could not have been killed: 'because it was not in the news. It was the same sort of game I played with myself on other days, for instance that Wednesday was our daughter Lisa's eleventh birthday and I had said to myself whatever happens it won't be on her birthday.' Weeks of anxiety had been exacerbated by her husband's recent posting to 45 Commando in Arbroath. Like the Evans family, Sue and Roger had decided to make their permanent home in the West Country. Sue was Devon-born and her family lived in Plymouth, so they had bought their own house just outside the city. Sue had had no plans for moving to Scotland with her daughters. When she rang Arbroath for news, she discovered she was not on their families list, and she still wonders how long it would have taken them to find her after Roger was killed if she had not taken it upon herself to phone them.

When she told the Marines she wanted her husband's body returned to her they said in effect 'No way,' but she persisted: 'He belonged to me. They took him away from me all those miles so they could bring him back.' Sue Enefer is a very determined lady, and the only time she thought she might not get her wish was when the widow of Lieutenant Colonel 'H' Jones, who was killed the day after Roger Enefer at Goose Green and posthumously awarded a VC, said she wanted her husband to remain where he was, buried with his men. After being part of Service life for twelve years, Sue knew the power of rank and precedence and thought: 'If the Colonel's widow says she wants her husband left out there they might use that as an excuse for not bringing any of the other men home.' And the week after the battle for Goose Green and Darwin, when it was announced that twelve of the seventeen soldiers, including Lieutenant Colonel 'H' Jones, had been buried in a mass grave, the Ministry of Defence, in response to further requests from bereaved relatives for the return of their men, blandly stated: 'It was a long-established custom and practice to bury British war dead on land or sea where they fell.' It was a practice that would eventually be reconsidered and changed, because of the stand by wives like Sue Enefer, who argued that according to Margaret Thatcher the Falklands was not supposed to be a war, and in similar circumstances, such as Northern Ireland, where her husband had done eleven tours, the Army did bring casualties back home for military burials.

Sue Enefer was told within twenty-four hours that her husband had died. She would later meet another widow whose Royal Marine husband was killed at the same time as Roger Enefer, but who was not told until two days later, though she had telephoned 45 Commando in Abroath after hearing a radio news item about Marine casualties and been reassured he was not one of them. A degree of human error is understandable in the chaos of the battlefield, but it is difficult to condone this particular mistake when the men were from the same company and were killed at the same time. It was the deliberate, supposedly strategic, delays in withholding news of casualties – and the inevitable rumours, leaks and confusion surrounding such tense and tragic occasions – that distressed thousands of families and later angered their men when they returned home and learned of the anxious days their relatives had lived through, not knowing *who* had been killed.

In retrospect, there seems no justification – strategic or otherwise – for the naval commanders at Fleet Headquarters banning John Nott from naming the HMS *Coventry* in his 'bad news' television bulletin on 25 May, while the later cover-up of the Bluff Cove casualties appears now to be even less legitimate. The three days delay in telling some families that their men were among those dead – a time-lag compounded by the Ministry of Defence's encouraging the press to speculate as they wished and, indeed, exaggerate the number of dead – is just another aspect of the most controversial incident in the whole Falklands War. On Tuesday 8 June, Argentine aircraft attacked the landing ships *Sir Galahad* and *Sir Tristram* at anchor in the waters of Fitzroy. On board the *Sir Galahad* were Guardsmen from the Prince of Wales Company, 3 Company, the mortar platoon and support echelon of the Welsh Guards, waiting to go ashore and join 2 Company and their battalion headquarters group at Bluff

Cove. Within one minute of the devastating bomb attack, thirty-eight Welsh Guards were killed and eighty-five wounded, some horribly burned. The final casualty figure of fifty-one dead included Royal Navy, Merchant Seamen and Army staff.

That same day in the Welsh Guards' married quarters at Pirbright, Jane Keoghane recalls hearing on a late night BBC2 television programme that a ship with Welsh Guards on board had been hit. She assumed that, as no one had contacted her, Kevin was not only safe but already ashore. The next day, when she spoke briefly to staff at the camp, she was assured there was nothing to worry about; although they had received information of casualties, Kevin was not listed. With the men away in the Falklands, many of the young wives staying with family and friends, and those who remained busy with jobs and school children, the atmosphere at the camp was quietly relaxed and low key; there was certainly no hint of the terrible tragedy in the South Atlantic. Jane was more concerned about whether Kevin would be home in time for the birth of their first child in September than the latest news of the war.

On Friday morning at 7.55, she was about to leave for her work as a community nurse with the local area health authority, when the camp's families' officer came to the front door with one of Jane's neighbours. The neighbour had been walking up the road when she saw the officer approaching Jane's house, intuitively guessed it was bad news and insisted on accompanying him. Jane believes, if it had not been for her, she would have been left alone after she had been told that Kevin was missing and that the officer would come back to see her later. 'He didn't even sit down, he just blurted it out and I was left standing on the doorstep. I was later told he had been very upset himself because two of his sons were out there and he did not know what had happened to them. But if that was how he was taking it he should not have been the one to come round and tell me my husband was missing; there should have been someone else doing the job, particularly someone with some experience in counselling.'

He did not appear to know or even notice that Jane was six months pregnant, although a camp doctor came later in the day to see if she needed anything. She contacted her family in

Newport, and Kevin's father, only to discover he had been told of his son's death at 7 am that morning. 'Someone from the battalion headquarters had phoned him out of courtesy because he was an ex-Welsh Guard.' The families' officer did not return that day and there was no further news until Saturday, when he called to say they must now presume Kevin was dead. At first Jane refused to believe him. A body would have been conclusive proof, and after the confusion during the week there was still a nagging doubt and, therefore, hope. On Sunday she left. At home in Wales there were her father, her sister, Rae, and brother, Bobby, and his family to care for and comfort her, but the shock of her husband's death was not lessened by the lack of interest shown in her abrupt departure. No one seemed to care about her whereabouts. 'What was so awful was the complete absence of someone from the Welsh Guards who knew how to cope with the situation. As a community nurse I know how vital support systems are to families who have experienced tragedy like a bereavement and yet the Armed Forces, whose business is life and death, do not have a system that can cope with the aftermath of a war. For me this inability to know what to do, how to behave, was even more shocking from the branch of the Services which prides itself on being a family regiment. I had always believed they would take care of their own, but it is a myth, it is rubbish.'

After weeks of expecting only bad news, Caroline Hailwood, whose husband Christopher was the third engineer on the *Sir Galahad*, switched on the BBC Radio 4 *Today* programme at 6.30 am on Wednesday 9 June and heard that two ships had been hit. For the first time since he was born, her six-month-old son, Jim, had lain awake all night. 'When the news came on the radio I thought, that is why.' She was quite calm when her father called round to see if she was all right. She had finally moved with the help of friends just five days before; the house was not yet on the telephone and Caroline had given her parents' number to her husband's office so they could contact them with any news. No one telephoned until Thursday, when the caller told Caroline's mother there was no news of Chris. After finishing her teaching that day Caroline left school to visit her parents, and she stopped off at a public call box to phone one of the emergency inquiry numbers broadcast for task force families; she wanted to make sure that they knew she had moved and that they had her parents' telephone number. When she arrived at her parents' house there was a man from the welfare department of the Royal Aircraft Establishment at Farnborough waiting to tell her that Chris was missing, presumed dead. 'He was a complete stranger, possibly the only Services welfare officer they could find living near me. He was very nice.'

Her parents would have preferred her to stay with them for a while, but Caroline told me how she had been so convinced Chris would not come back that it was almost a relief to begin thinking of other things, and she wanted to make sure that Jim had a reassuring routine in the familiar surroundings of their own home. She even returned to her job the following week, although her headmaster advised her to take it a day at a time and did not expect her to turn up for classes if she did not feel up to teaching. Getting herself out of the house in the morning, and Jim to his child minder, combined with the company of colleagues who overwhelmed her with offers of help and kindness, was an essential part of restoring some sort of normality to her life. Only her weight loss from eight-and-a-half to just under seven stone revealed what she really felt about what had happened to her husband of twenty months, who had been as horrified as his young wife at so unexpected a turn of events in his career as an engineer on a non-combatant civilian supply ship.

The weekend after Bluff Cove was the last in the Argentine occupation of the islands and the 3rd Battalion Parachute Regiment were detailed to take the 600-foot heights of Mount Longdon, five miles west of Stanley. During the night of 11/12 June, Ian McKay, the platoon sergeant for 4 Platoon B Company, was killed in an action for which he was posthumously awarded one of the war's two Victoria Crosses. After a ten-hour battle the final casualty list for 3 Para was twenty-three soldiers killed and forty-seven injured.

At the married quarters in Aldershot on Monday morning, it was left to Sue Patton, wife of Major Roger Patton, second in command of 3 Para, to break the news to the widows, including Marica McKay, who says little about that time other than: 'Everyone was very good, Sue just told me he had died and I did not ask for details, I could not see the point, Ian was dead.' Fourteen days later, when visiting a friend, she was shown a blow-by-blow account by reporter Max Hastings in the *Sunday Express* which described the engagement in which Ian was killed, and how he was killed. It was a shock to read it in black and white.

Marica had been born into an Army family. As a child she lived with her parents in Aden and Bengazi and she was educated at a boarding school in Malta before training as a dental nurse with the Queen Alexandra's Royal Army Nursing Corps. Her first husband, Bill Coffey, the father of her teenage son Donny, is a sergeant major in the Paras, a regiment Donny cannot wait to join too. Aldershot, the Paras' home-base, has been her only home since she came to England when she was seventeen, and although Ian occasionally talked about leaving the Army, she knew it was just talk. Neither of them liked the separations because of his work, Ian particularly after the birth of their daughter Melanie, who was five that year. 'You would never have thought anyone had had a daughter before Ian, people used to talk about how he idolised her.' For the previous two years he had really enjoyed his role as an instructor at the Aldershot Barracks and Marica was reconciled to being an Army wife until he retired. She describes herself as an old hand at coping with the Armed Forces' attitudes to families, but in the months that followed her husband's death even she was surprised on occasions by the behaviour of the Services to widows and soldiers injured in the Falklands, behaviour she summarises as: 'Wives and families are excess baggage and the only interest the Services have in you is what your husband does. If you lose your husband you not only lose your status, but your way of life, and eventually your home if you live in married quarters.' It was something she had never really thought about because she had never known any other way of life, just as: 'I never thought about Ian dying; you just don't believe it is going to happen to you.'

CHAPTER THREE:

The Armed Forces' response to women's needs

'I was not the only widow expecting a baby. The Welsh Guards were supposed to explain all the financial arrangements to me. Nobody ever came.' Widow Jane Keoghane.

After the death of Kevin, his widow, Jane Keoghane, was acutely aware of her sudden isolation. For six years she had been part of a world very different from ordinary civilian life, an exclusive society with its own history, customs, uniforms, and a rank structure as rigid as a caste system, in which wives are permitted social roles only and the places allotted them in the all-male hierarchy depend very much on their husbands' positions in the regiment. Most women no longer see their marital status in such conventional terms but it is difficult to break a mould when a system is enforced from the top by an inflexible order of command. To challenge it causes not only embarrassment to the woman's husband, but possible reprimand from a senior officer for allowing his wife 'to step out of line'. In some regiments a non-conscript generation of Servicemen has tried to change attitudes to wives and families, but the chauvinism that still exists in the Armed Forces is very much out of date with the social changes that have taken place in most women's lives in the past twenty years.

Jane Keoghane, who had her own career as a community nurse, did not personally depend on her husband's rank as a Lance Sergeant in the Welsh Guards for her social identity, but as a widow she no longer had a legitimate role in the Armed Forces, and to be excluded from a way of life at the same time as losing a husband was doubly difficult to adjust to. Jane had belonged to a regiment that prides itself on being a 'family', where some wives speak of how many years they, rather than their husbands, have been in the Welsh Guards. She lost her place in this close-knit community.

It is not surprising that women widowed by the Falklands War do feel very differently about their widowhood from women whose husbands have died in other circumstances. In addition to the unexpected nature of their husbands' deaths, the behaviour of the Service in which their husbands gave their lives has very much contributed to how they have come to terms with their widowhood. The way some now feel about their circumstances, and the war itself, is often attributable to the manner in which the different Armed Forces handled their bereavement. Many discovered that the Services' approach to the domestic consequences of war has not altered much since the Second World War. While the Welfare State has eradicated much of the poverty of earlier generations the attitudes to war widows and a woman's role in Service life have not radically changed since: 'Officers' wives ate puddings and pies and squaddies' wives ate skilly.'

Colonel's wife Meg Baxter believes that wives of soldiers, whatever their rank, are part of their husbands' jobs; that it is not like being married to a bank manager whose wife perhaps only visits his work place once a year for the office party. Armed Forces personnel work, socialise, live next door to each other; their homes in married quarters belong to the Services, so do their furniture and their non-civilian clothes. 'Wives and children belong to them too in a way, we are all part of one big family.' As a senior officer's wife, Meg is expected to assume certain responsibilities towards the families of her husband's soldiers and she, too, feels that because of her husband's rank it is her 'duty' to know what is happening to them and to help and advise in any way. Whereas the Royal Navy has a paternal approach to Service welfare, reinforced by the exclusive male society on board ship, the Army views its separate operational units in terms of families. 'The Commanding Officer is the father and his wife is mum,' says Meg Baxter. Soldiers' wives, especially officers' wives, are expected to make their husbands' jobs their number one priority and there is a social stigma attached to those who don't pull their weight and help their man. But that help is strictly confined to social roles; the Services still insist that the men be allowed to do their work without any domestic intrusion, even if the wife thinks she can contribute something professionally to her husband's career. Meg feels that such limitations are unrealistic given the different generation of women now in the Services. 'We are no longer just camp followers. We are better educated, more articulate, and want to be kept informed about our husbands' work. We expect to have control too over our own destinies, particularly as a lot of wives are professionally qualified and want to pursue their own careers.'

At one posting before moving to Plymouth, Meg had been the temporary head of a girls' private school; in Devon she is a freelance journalist and broadcaster, although her work is very much circumscribed by 'not doing anything that would embarrass the Services'. Other Service wives deliberately choose professions like nursing, teaching and social work – jobs for which there is some prospect of employment in the Services themselves.

In some Army units there is occasionally a more informal social mix between the ranks and their families because of the initiatives of individual Commanding Officers. The impact of the Falklands War on the Service families in Plymouth accelerated – if only temporarily – that trend, especially among the women. It was certainly noticeable among Royal Navy personnel, who are by far the most formal of the three Services. Over 12,000 men from the Plymouth area were despatched to the war in the South Atlantic, the largest number of task force personnel from any one city in Britain. Operation Corporate was an unscheduled departure from the normal routine of Service life; it was unlike any other military exercise, with dates for return ringed in diaries and on calenders.

The problems of temporarily becoming one-parent families are common to all ranks in the Armed Forces, and some parents try to minimise the effects by sending their children to boarding schools. Wives and children have to adjust to regular separations which – in the case of tours of Northern Ireland or an overseas posting such as Belize – can last a number of months. It is not only difficult for young children to cope with the sudden absence of their father, but for newly married wives and first-time mothers separations can be traumatic. It is a way of life that few civilian families would choose and Meg Baxter has noticed, during twenty years teaching in both State and Service schools, that there is a higher level of dyslexia among Service children. 'Unfortunately you also get what I call "the wooden spoon syndrome", where a mum left on her own takes out her problems on the children, and this can happen in any family, regardless of rank.' In the late Spring and early Summer of 1982 thousands of wives and children living in the West Country were left to cope alone and, with the remaining Service staff stretched to the limit, it was often officers' wives who assumed social and welfare responsibilities for these families.

In Plymouth the local community response to the Falklands War was perhaps appropriate in a city whose skyline is dominated by a massive memorial to the Second World War; it was the spirit of the blitz, during which Plymouth was almost razed to the ground. Meg Baxter recalls: 'There was a great breaking down of barriers between the civic and Service personnel, and within the Armed Forces far more contact with other ranks than there had ever been. Navy officers' wives actually went along to community centres and socialised with ranks they had never met before, everyone was very much involved with what was happening.'

The formalities of Royal Navy life were an aspect of Chief Petty Officer Edmund Flanagan's work that often exasperated Anita during their eighteen-year marriage and the nine different married quarters his postings took them to. Officers' accommodation is invariably separate from and superior to that provided for families of Naval ratings and the divisions of residential areas on the basis of rank does little to encourage a mixed social life. Anita observed that those wives who 'pulled' their husbands' ranks on others were the ones who had tended to marry soon after leaving school, had no professional qualifications or jobs, sent their children to boarding schools and regarded the social round of coffee mornings, voluntary work, bridge parties and entertaining and being entertained as a full-time job. 'They are the sort who don't mix socially with the wives of other ranks in the NAAFI and, on formal occasions like a dance, don't expect the lower ranks to take to the floor until the officers and their ladies have had a dance.' Anita, who combined her work as a nurse with bringing up four children, had neither the personality nor the time for such formalities. One of her friends was the wife of a Royal Navy cook and they visited each other in their respective married quarters with no social inhibitions until their husbands returned from sea and the cook made it clear to his wife that he did not like her going to a Chief Petty Officer's home. When Anita invited the couple round for a meal the cook's wife explained that her husband did not think such an occasion would be socially appropriate. Edmund Flanagan short-circuited the impasse by going round to the cook's home and 'ordering' him to dinner. 'Once we had got over that hurdle it was a perfectly relaxed relationship. Edmund and my friend's husband would often go out for a pint together.'

Despite the paternalism of the Royal Navy, Anita has nothing but praise for individual welfare and family officers who helped sort out her financial and personal affairs after her husband died on the *Atlantic Conveyor*. The Flanagans' eldest son, Grant had already left school and started work when his father was killed. After much discussion, and with the enthusiastic approval of her younger children, Cassandra and Tarquin, Anita decided to accept the Royal Navy's offer of places at a co-educational boarding school for them. The family officer who suggested the move arranged for the fees to be paid by the Nore Trust, a charity which helps educate children of Royal Navy and Merchant Navy personnel who have lost one or both parents. Anita's next priority was to find a house of her own. She was anxious to move before Christmas, as the married quarters on the private estate in Rainham held memories made more poignant when her neighbours' husbands all returned home safely from the South Atlantic. There was no pressure on her to leave the Service accommodation, although three months after Edmund died she received a formal notice to vacate the premises by 6 January, and her rent receipts were amended to the 'illegal occupancy of a married quarter', which the Naval welfare officer hastily reassured her was just a formality used by the Services for those occupying Ministry of Defence property after the legal tenant, a Serviceman, had died. After a brief return to her nursing job at a local hospital, Anita left to move in November to Gillingham. It was the first home she could call her own, purchased with various monies paid because of the death of her husband in the South Atlantic.

Maureen Emly was married five years before the birth of her only child, Matthew, and her husband Richard's career in the Royal Navy had always come before anything else. Sub Lieutenant Emly was an ambitious electronics specialist who had studied hard for his commission. While Maureen enjoyed being at home with their son, she also regarded her role as Richard's wife as 'a sort of job', moving around to different postings, creating new homes, making new friends. It was a way of life which she felt made it difficult for her to have a separate career, put down roots, or make long-standing friends. Although they had only recently bought their own home in Portsmouth, Maureen was prepared to move the family and start again if her husband had got the Washington post he had applied for before going to the Falklands. Richard and six-year-old Matthew were her whole life, her only close family being her widowed sister, Pat, and their father, who lived in London. She will always remember the individual kindness of some of her husband's colleagues after the *Sheffield* was hit and Richard died. She received a telegram from Captain Sam Salt while he was on his way home with the other *Sheffield* survivors, and the wife of Richard's previous Captain visited her. When the *Sheffield*'s crew returned to Britain late in May, some of the men who had been with Richard, and whom she had met during her husband's brief one-week shore leave in Athens that March, came to see her. 'It was very difficult for them but a tremendous help to me, talking about what had happened. Sam Salt came round to lunch. He was very kind and it was quite informal, he brought his dog with him.'

She contrasts the concern of individuals with a system that automatically on the death of her husband closed his charge account in the officers' wardroom at HMS *Nelson*, Portsmouth, which meant she could no longer use the facilities. When she asked if it was possible to drop in and have a drink or meal with friends, as she had done before when Richard was at sea, putting her bill on his account, she was told wives could not hold accounts in their own right and the system did not allow for cash payments. 'I began to realise just how different the Services were from civilian life. I had lost my husband so I had no identity any more. The Royal Navy did not accept me as a person in my own right.' Later she had to ask for an invitation for Matthew to go with his friends to the local Royal Navy Christmas party, as he did not automatically receive one as he had done the previous year. Apart from the Royal Navy welfare office who tried to do a means test on her for the South Atlantic Fund, no one called to see her about her personal welfare or to discuss Matthew's future and his education. 'I was just left to get on with it. If it had not been for my sister, Pat, I do not know how I would have coped.'

Lynda Gallagher would have found the formalities of Royal Navy life incomprehensible. Although her SAS husband was a sergeant major, one of her closest friends is the young widow of a trooper. 'Rank never made any difference to the wives in the first place, and in circumstances like these it is immaterial.' The commanding officer from Lawrence Gallagher's squadron used to come to their home with his wife for informal lunches, and expected Lynda and her husband to drop in on him and his family in the same way. Lynda's husband had teased her that she was lucky he was in the Special Air Services, as she would not have taken too kindly to the social expectations of different ranks in other regiments, and from the experiences of two of her nephews in the Grenadier Guards, she knows exactly what he meant. 'That is the regiment that is still known as the "pride and the poverty", and those boys certainly know their place. But in the SAS there is no snobbery because of rank. Sometimes you get the occasional Rupert, usually an officer who has been seconded from a more traditional regiment who expects the men to know their place. They may call him "sir" but they feel no differently about him than the others, and newcomers soon get the message.'

Two SAS sergeant majors were killed in the helicopter crash in which Lawrence Gallagher died on 19 May, the remainder were from lower ranks, but almost all the wives who had lived in Hereford for any length of time knew each other. Their friendship and their social integration in a

50

civilian community from which many of them came (many, like Lynda, had parents and relatives living nearby) was a tremendous help in the first months of their bereavement. Lynda recalls how they sat in each others homes and talked about what had happened to them 'a million times', without the inhibition they might be boring or upsetting. 'It was a great comfort that we could share our grief without any embarrassment.' Equally important was the quick response from the regiment's family officer and paymaster, who were concerned they should have no immediate financial problems or money worries about the future. Both men spent hours patiently explaining the financial position, how best to plan moneywise for the future, and both helped with the inevitable volume of paperwork and form-filling. Lynda will always be grateful for their advice at a time when her grief was compounded by worries about bringing up single-handed two little girls and the baby she was expecting. As a pregnant mother, there was the trauma of having to adjust to being referred to as a widow: 'The very day after they told me Lawrence had died I got a cheque for £1,650 from our insurance company, The Scottish Widows. I realise in these circumstances they are concerned we should not have to worry about money, but so soon after the news just the idea of being called a widow seemed unreal.'

The night the commanding officer of Lawrence Gallagher's unit returned from the Falklands, he personally visited all the regiment's widows. Lawrence's best friend also came that evening. But other soldiers they knew stayed away for a while, 'perhaps because they were embarrassed or too nervous to know what to say to me'. It was the regiment's worst single tragedy since its formation in 1942. Once the immediate impact receded, and a return to their more routine role minimised the initial shock, the SAS honoured their dead with a plaque in the local parish church of St Martin's and memorial vases with individually chosen stone-engraved messages from each of the bereaved families. The vases are not just a place for flowers but a setting where the widows and their families can remember the men whose bodies were never recovered. The regiment also topped up the £63,000 given by the people of Hereford to the soldiers' wives, so that each widow eventually received £5,000. The response by such a small unit, famed for its aggressive professionalism and unorthodox and highly individual behaviour, was a contrast to that of more traditional regiments.

Jane Keoghane had never paid much attention to the formalities of Service life, although she does admit that the rank system matters socially: 'If you were not in with the senior warrant officers' wives you could have a bad time at social events. But Kevin was very popular, and we both enjoyed volunteering to help out at mess functions.' Jane feels that, because her career as a nurse is one which is acceptable to the Services, and it is also a uniformed profession, she was treated a bit differently from other wives, who often sought her advice because of her medical experience and her age (at thirty-two, she was older than many of the teenage brides of her husband's young soldiers). 'So in some ways I was not only Kevin's wife but I was a person in my own right.'

In spite of her independence, Jane was proud of her husband's professionalism as a career soldier, but both of them were aware of the disruptive effects the regular moves and the separations had on children, and had planned the birth of their first baby to coincide with Jane leaving work and setting up a home away from married quarters. After the tragedy of Bluff Cove, there was no point in delaying. She went to stay with her widowed father in their home town of Newport and, with the baby due in September, was anxious to establish her own place, preferably on the same council estate as her father and sister, Rae. She twice returned briefly to Pirbright camp to collect her personal belongings. Her brother, Bobby, later cleared the remainder of her possessions from the married quarters, and made sure the camp's families' officer knew his sister's temporary address to forward mail and Kevin's papers. From the moment she left Pirbright the regiment always knew where Jane was, but no one took the initiative to get in touch, or see if she had any problems or needed help in any way.

'While the regiment's lack of interest in me was distressing, it was as though they no longer wanted to know me.' Jane describes subsequent events as 'a chapter of nightmares'. She discovered that her husband was retrospectively taken off the payroll the day after he died on 8 June, although it had been four days before she was officially told he must be presumed dead. She was then twenty-six weeks pregnant, but, in accordance with Service pay codes, as a childless widow she received only 91 days of Kevin's full pay, instead of the 182 days awarded widows with children. No one called to explain her complicated financial status as a war-widowed pregnant woman until a war pension officer visited her at her father's home in July to discuss the weekly £38.45 war widow's pension. There was no mention of the £22.50 maternity benefit or the £41.40 widow's allowance she was already receiving from the Department of Health and Social Security. On 10 August a male officer from the local DHSS office called on Jane and, in the presence of her sister, insisted on taking away her maternity and widow's allowance books, telling her she could be charged with fraud for claiming all three benefits. The following day a woman DHSS official from the same office called to return her maternity allowance book and explained that Jane did not qualify for the full widow's allowances while in receipt of the maternity benefit. From total weekly benefits of £102.35 the sum was almost halved to £58. After the statutory eighteen weeks' maternity benefit had been paid both widow's allowances were restored in full. The indignity of the experience still rankles: 'I was not the only widow expecting a baby. The Welsh Guards were supposed to arrange for someone to come from Maindy Barracks in Cardiff and explain all this to me, but nobody ever came.'

When Jane needed to trace Kevin's will, which had been deposited with his regiment's pay office, her sister phoned the Welsh Guards headquarters in Birdcage Walk, London, and was referred to the Ministry of Defence Estates Office. Jane received the will and at the same time two photostat copies were sent to her father and Kevin's father; when she asked why her husband's will had been opened without permission from his next of kin, she was told it was usual to mail copies to executors nominated by the person making the will, but, as she says: 'They did not know who they were until they opened the will.' When Jane received a month's rent bill for £46.20 for the unoccupied quarter in Pirbright, her decision to refuse to pay it on principle led to a letter from the Command Pay Office UK Land Forces, Worthy Down, Winchester, warning if the bill was not settled within twenty-eight days the case would be referred to their solicitor. Jane forwarded the letter to the Welsh Guards headquarters in London and, after a telephone call from them to say it had been dealt with, heard no more, not even an apology or explanation.

One response from the Welsh authorities to the disaster in Bluff Cove in which thirty-eight Welsh Guards had died was an offer from some councils to re-house widows near their families, if there was suitable property vacant. Although Newport did not actually make such an offer, Jane knew one young widow who had been given the keys by Taff-Ely council on 21 June – just two weeks after her husband's death – to a brand new council house on her father-in-law's doorstep. Jane had returned to Newport in the hope of living on or near the same estate as her father and sister. When her family called the local housing department about the possibility of Jane being allocated one of the two houses already vacant on the estate, they were told she would have to go on the waiting list, that a house might not be available for three to nine *years*, and there was no guarantee of one within the same neighbour-hood. After a number of appeals, Mrs Keoghane was classi-fied a homeless person, which meant the local authority had a statutory duty to re-house her immediately, and she was eventually offered one of the empty houses on the same estate as her family, a home she is now buying for herself and her son, Philip.

The cumulative muddle of Jane Keoghane's experiences is an irony in a society whose Prime Minister referred to all Servicemen in the Falklands as 'our boys', in which national newspapers headlined every soldier in the South Atlantic 'a hero' and regimental officers were already penning recom-mendations for medals. The bill for Operation Corporate, the replacement cost of task force ships lost in the war, the government's policy of turning the islands into a permanently garrisoned fortress, would run into billions of pounds. But what price a Type 42 destroyer or a new military airport compared with a rent demand for £40 odd on an unoccu-pied married quarter vacated on the death of a soldier in Bluff Cove, the one tragic incident in the whole war that could possibly have been avoided? And just what sort of mealy-mouthed system awards 91 days' full pay to a newly widowed woman, six months pregnant with her first child, when, had the tragedy been twelve weeks later, she would have qualified with a new-born baby for 182 days pay?

The initial stone-walling that met Jane Keoghane's request to buy a home near her family where she could bring up her unborn child was not so very different from those councils who refused to put Second World War widows on their housing waiting lists because they had no husbands. The punitive threat implicit behind a DHSS official's talk of possible fraud because a woman had unwittingly claimed overlapping benefits is reminiscent of a society that, a generation ago, allowed impoverished war widows to place their children in orphanages so they could go out to work, and, once they became wage-earners, savagely taxed their widow's pensions. Perhaps the silence from a regiment which made no move to inquire about the welfare of a soldier's widow is to be expected in a society that treats over 65,000 Servicemen's wives, widowed before 1973, as second-class widows. 1973 was the year additional payments were made by the Ministry of Defence to women widowed by their husbands' deaths in Northern Ireland; subsequent increases on that initial sum mean Service wives widowed since now receive pensions almost double those of pre-1973 war widows, who are paid only the DHSS pension. No wonder a seventy-year-old war widow like Muriel Nicolson was last year reduced to selling her RAF pilot husband's Battle of Britain Victoria Cross to ease her poverty. The auction price on the regimental silver in half a dozen mess rooms in the Armed Forces would probably wipe out the money problems of Mrs Nicolson and her contemporaries, whose only alternative is a means-tested handout from a Service charity. No other European country regards its World War Two widows with such contempt, so perhaps it was not so surprising that a Falklands War widow should have been treated in a less than compassionate manner.

At least some of the financial provisions from various sources for Falklands War widows were economically more realistic in 1982. Ministry of Defence figures for tax-free death grants, including an additional gratuity paid for death directly attributable to Service, as in the Falklands, listed the widow of a private soldier being paid, according to his length of service, between £7,500 and £10,500, a sergeant's widow £10,250 to

£14,500, the widow of a captain from £14,500 to £20,500, and a colonel's widow from £25,500 to £35,500. Although war widows' pensions from the DHSS are now tax-free, the additional Ministry of Defence pensions are taxed, but index-linked, and far from generous for childless widows. A private soldier's widow under forty with no children received joint pensions in 1982 of £2,700 per annum, a sergeant's widow £3,700, a captain's £5,300 and a colonel's £9,200. Additional payments from the DHSS and the Ministry of Defence for two dependent children would increase those sums respectively to private – £6,500, sergeant – £8,000, captain – £10,000 and colonel – £15,900.

Jane Keoghane says it was not money worries that upset her but the absence of anyone who knew how to handle her affairs with any degree of confidence or compassion. There did not appear to be any rule book covering her conditions as a homeless, war-widowed, expectant mother; there was no one to talk to; and the attitude of those from whom she sought practical and financial advice 'was most distressing'. Emotionally, the reaction was more thoughtful: when the Welsh Guards returned home, Kevin's surviving friends visited her; the regiment sent flowers on the birth of his son, Philip; and the battalion's Colonel, John Rickett, called on Jane and her baby in hospital.

Jane Keoghane's sense of isolation was only too familiar to Dorothy Foulkes. Twelve men died when the *Atlantic Conveyor* was bombed on 25 May; six of them, including Frank Foulkes and the ship's Captain, Ian North, were regular crew who had volunteered for Operation Corporate, and they left three widows. As one of those widows Dorothy feels that the families of the merchant seamen volunteers 'were left at the bottom of everybody's list. My husband was working for the Ministry of Defence and his country. Cunard made a great patriotic fuss about their ships and volunteer crew going to war, but when Frank died I might have well not existed.'

On the day Dorothy was told of Frank's death by a stranger from the Manchester office of the Missions for Seamen, she was visited by a personnel administrator from Cunard. Dorothy, the mother of six children with three girls still at home, asked the administrator about her husband's pension and company insurance, and she was told that these would have to be investigated because Frank had not died on company business but 'in a war-type situation'. Dorothy told me: 'For a month I was worried stupid about money; there seemed no guarantee they would automatically pay up.' When an official from Frank's seaman's union called on the family he promised to sort out Mrs Foulkes' finances, but offered no immediate help or advice. A neighbour, who knew an employee in the local Department of Health and Social Security pensions department, asked for someone to visit Dorothy with details on her widow's pension. It was Dorothy's daughter, Angela, who lived in Germany with her Royal Signal Corps husband, who, some weeks later, realised her mother qualified for the tax-free war widow's pension from the DHSS and got her to change her pension book.

After a fortnight's compassionate leave from her Army civilian job, Angela returned to Germany still concerned about her mother and younger sisters. She talked about the situation with one of her senior officers and the Brigadier promptly telephoned the Ministry of Defence in London, who, in turn, immediately contacted Cunard. The same day, Dorothy received a call from the London office to reassure her they were dealing with the formalities, although there was no explanation or apology for the delay. Dorothy's RAF son, David, had also been told by his warrant officer that his mother should get in touch with them if she needed any help or advice, but she felt it was Cunard's responsibility to handle their employees' affairs. She still wonders how they could have been so inept when she learned that another Cunard widow, Valerie Hughes, whose husband had been the *Atlantic Conveyor*'s engineer, had been told within days of her husband's death of the financial arrangements for herself and three daughters by a representative from their London office, who visited her in Gosport to say it was only a matter of time before the company authorised the payment of insurance and a pension. When Dorothy met Mrs Hughes after the St Paul's Falklands memorial service on 26 July, she was surprised to learn that Cunard had also offered help with educating her daughters by arranging for private school fees to be paid for by a Service charity. Wanting to know why her two school-age daughters, Victoria and Charlotte, had not been offered the same opportunity, their mother approached Cunard and the secretary of the Royal Merchant Navy School, Bearwood College, near Reading, phoned her to say no one had told them Frank Foulkes had any children. The secretary visited the family the following January, but the two girls decided they did not want to be parted from their ponies, who were stabled near their home, and opted to go as day pupils to a local private school. Their fees are paid for by the Bearwood-based charity, who, Dorothy says: 'have been very kind, and were amazed no one had told them about us at the beginning.'

The St Paul's memorial service for the Falklands casualties on 26 July was the first opportunity many of the bereaved families had of meeting each other and Servicemen who had returned from the South Atlantic. It was an emotional occasion and the conciliatory sermon by Robert Runcie, Archbishop of Canterbury, was not well received by the triumphal Margaret Thatcher.

At one of the buffet lunches for the mourners attended by senior Armed Forces personnel, Caroline Hailwood, whose Fleet Auxiliary husband, Christopher, had been the third engineer on the landing ship, the *Sir Galahad*, button-holed Rear Admiral Kenneth Wilcockson, Director of Navy Personnel Services. He had recently been appointed by John Nott as one of the trustees of the publicly subscribed South Atlantic Fund. It had been six weeks since Caroline's husband had died and no one had been to see her about financial arrangements. The only money she had received was a £100 DHSS death grant, which she describes as 'funeral expenses, despite the fact Chris had been lost at sea'. When she read a newspaper report that the South Atlantic Fund was intending to give the Falklands widows £10,000 each, she telephoned the paper for more details and told a journalist she had received nothing other than the statutory state handout. The paper published Caroline's story and another covering her conversation with Rear Admiral Wilcockson, who was taken aback that she had been given nothing other than the DHSS £100. The following day a cheque for £1,650 arrived in the post from the National Maritime Board, an insurance sum payable on death in Service to the next of kin. Included with it were details of Christopher's pension from the Ministry of Defence, who were very cross at the newspaper publicity. No one had been in touch to explain that the delay was probably due to Christopher not having signed a death benefit form or made a will. But Caroline and her baby son Jim were obviously the only beneficiaries. She explained to me that all payments had been withheld until she got probate: 'Fortunately I did not have any immediate money problems, I had a job, our own home, and my parents lived nearby. But what if I had been hard up? Who would I have turned to? No one came to me. I even doubt if one of the Service charities could have given me anything as Christopher was not a member of the Armed Forces.'

Caroline remembered her husband telling her that for nine years he had bought gifts from the annual King George's Fund for Sailors Christmas catalogue because he believed that was the charity which looked after all men who went to sea. That mid-September, when she received their 1982 Christmas catalogue addressed to her husband, she wrote to ask if they could tell her of any provisions she and her son might be entitled to. She describes their response in a letter dated 8 October as 'snooty'. When the monies began to arrive from different sources, a covering letter with a cheque from the South Atlantic Fund suggested if any financial advice was needed she consult her welfare officer. 'I didn't have a welfare officer, I am not in the Services. In the end I got my bank to sort it all out.'

Caroline described to me how she felt that in some respects her isolation from other bereaved families helped her adjust to her situation quicker than if she had been part of a Service life which, in her changed circumstances as a widow, she would have had to leave behind. The one occasion when she and her parents felt the need to 'belong' to something more than their civilian lives, and feel closer to the events in the South Atlantic, was the memorial service. Caroline's parents come from Newport, her father's family are Welsh speakers and many of them have served with the Welsh Guards. When her father heard of the memorial service that was being arranged at Llandaff Cathedral for the thirty-eight Welsh Guardsmen who had died on the *Sir Galahad* at the same time as his son-in-law, he wanted to attend, not only to pay his respects to Christopher but also to his fellow countrymen who had died in the service of a regiment he was proud of. He wrote to the Welsh Guards headquarters in London, explaining his request for permission to attend with his wife and widowed daughter. He never received a reply. The Sunday before the service, Caroline had a telephone call from the wife of the *Sir Galahad*'s captain saying they had been invited to the service and, if she was going, could probably get a lift from one of the coaches taking families from Pirbright Barracks. Caroline phoned Pirbright and was told she could certainly have a lift, but they had better check with Maindy Barracks, Cardiff, if the Hailwood party had been allocated seats in the Cathedral. There was no record of her father's request and no spare seats were available. At school the next day she found it difficult to settle down and phoned Pirbright just before midday to see if there had been any last-minute changes; when she was told they had heard nothing, she decided to go home for lunch. Waiting on her front doorstep was a crewman from the *Sir Galahad* whom Chris had introduced her to just before he left for the Falklands. He did not really know why he had come that particular day, but he just felt he had to see her and tell her what had happened to them on 8 June in Bluff Cove. Caroline remembers: 'It was just an extraordinary coincidence that he turned up when he did, he was only a kid and in a terrible state.'

It had been a long, strained day when the wife of the *Sir Galahad* captain phoned later to say how disappointed they were that Caroline and her parents had been unable to make the service, as seats had been allotted them next to her and her husband. At one o'clock someone had phoned Caroline's school to tell her she and her parents could go after all, but even if they had received the message it would have been impossible to make the two-and-a-half hour journey in time for the service. On the surface the incident was no more than a series of bureaucratic blunders, but in the circumstances it left Caroline upset and angry, and her father feeling badly snubbed by the Welsh Guards. While individuals who knew Caroline Hailwood did all they could to help, when it came to her dealings with the Ministry of Defence, 'a faceless government department, or a set-up like the South Atlantic Fund, you are just a number. That is how the Services look upon their men and that is how they regard their families.'

60

It was a need to share their common grief and a feeling of alienation from the normal routine of Service life that brought together Royal Marine widows Sue Enefer and June Evans. Although they lived within half-an-hour's drive of each other, separated by the Tamar estuary that divides the Devon dockyard city of Plymouth from Cornwall, they had never met and neither of them knew other women whose husbands were Falklands casualties. During the weeks after Sergeant Roger Enefer's death on 27 May, Sue's nearby family, her friends and neighbours had rarely left her and daughters, Lisa and Donna, alone. A week or so after being told of her helicopter pilot husband's death on 21 May, June Evans had left her home in Landrake, Cornwall, and taken her children, Mark and Samantha, to stay with her brother in Accrington. After a month away from work, she returned to her job as a clerical officer in Devonport dockyard. June enjoyed her career and was ready for promotion when her husband, Sergeant Andy Evans, was killed. She had worked throughout their marriage, having left home at seventeen when her mother died and first arrived in Plymouth as a nineteen-year-old bride, whose soldier husband was posted to Northern Ireland three weeks after their wedding. She had not known anyone then, but found work and soon made friends, and now hoped that, having been so self-sufficient as a teenager and having later handled a full-time job and two children in her husband's absence, she would adjust more easily to being a widow.

The first few days back at work were made difficult by the sight and sound of helicopters in Devonport dockyard, but once she had accepted their presence and overcome the initial inhibitions of some colleagues who did not quite know what to say until June made the first move, she hoped a return to everyday routine would help her settle down. But for twelve years she had been the wife of a Royal Marine; it was the only life she knew as an adult. 'You cannot just put it aside. I had got used to the separations and being on my own, but there was always a date for Andy's return. This time there was nothing to look forward to, and how could I continue to be part of Andy's world? There was no going back to the old routines, I had to make a new life for myself and the children and I felt utterly alone.' There were days she could not believe

Andy was not coming back and one evening, returning home in her car from work, she followed a familiar motorbike, convinced the rider was her husband and was amazed when it went past their turning.

At her Plymstock home, Sue, who had temporarily given up her part-time work in a local school canteen, was experiencing similar feelings. Peter Humphries, the local welfare officer for the Royal Marines, had helped her with financial advice and form-filling, and listened sympathetically to her insistence that her husband's body be brought back to England for reburial. 'I would never accept Roger was not coming back until I had buried him. Only then would I believe it was final and could look to the future.' Sue, too, felt completely cut off from her late husband's world, particularly as she knew no one from his last posting to 45 Commando, Arbroath, as he had only moved there a month before the invasion of the Falklands. Once she had known Roger's unit had landed on the islands, she wrote two letters a day and, for weeks, carried her last unposted letter in her handbag, not knowing what to do with it. The Friday morning she had been told of Roger's death, she had received three letters from him in the same post. A month later, five arrived together, including two for Lisa and Donna. Soon after that her own letters started to return. She could not bring herself to tell the Post Office she did not want them. She needed to know which ones Roger had read, what news he had known of those waiting for him at home before he died. The post that brought five letters revealed how he had received a big greetings card Lisa's schoolfriends had made him, and a little sweet Donna had stuck inside her envelope for her father. The girls thought it wonderful he had got their mail, but Sue rang Peter Humphries in tears. He said it might help if she spoke to someone in the same circumstances and gave her June's work number. After their first hesitant conversation they talked on the phone almost every day and discovered similarities in their lives which made them feel they had more in common than their grief.

Both women had their thirty-first birthdays that year, their children were the same age, they shared the same wedding anniversary of 1 August, and had been married twelve years to their soldier husbands. In retrospect, these were trivial coincidences, but they helped bond their need to identify with someone facing up to the same unpredicted tragedy in their lives. Sue found a photograph of her husband taken in 1973 on a corporal's training course and among the names listed underneath was an Evans, whom June confirmed was her husband. The men stood within touching distance of each other. By comparing dates, their widows realised that Roger and Andy must have got to know each other well while part of a seven-man group on a senior command course at the Royal Marine training camp at Lympstone in 1980. The knowledge that their husbands had spent time in each other's company on happier occasions made the women feel even closer; the comfort of shared grief was the same as that experienced by Lynda Gallagher and other SAS widows in Hereford, but their friendship meant something more. The Royal Marines had been part of their lives too; as Sue told me: 'You tag along because it is your husband's job, but it was very hard after Roger died, losing not only him but a way of life. June and I could talk about things that mean little to other people outside the Services and try and help each other get over the fact we were no longer part of it.'

They met for the first time on an emotion-packed day when the requisitioned Cunard liner, the *Canberra*, returned to Southampton on Sunday 11 July, with the men from their husbands' units on board. With her two children, June drove through Plymouth with its carnival atmosphere of street parties, flags and bunting, and crowds with homemade 'Welcome Home' placards waiting for the coaches bringing the task force men from Southampton. The Royal Marine husband of one of Sue's neighbours on the estate where the Enefers were buying their own home was also expected home that day, but, aware of how Sue must be feeling, his family did not put out their flags and kept their celebration as quiet as possible. As Sue watched the television pictures of the troops disembarking, it was Roger's unit, 45 Commando, who came off the *Canberra* first, and his widow could not stop herself willing him to be there too. In the afternoon the women found their children in an upstairs bedroom watching the coaches with the returning Servicemen on the traffic-packed A38 road above the estate leading into Plymouth. Through the open window came the cheers of people lining the route and it was obvious that the children desperately wanted to join in. In the end they all went and cheered, and the women wished they, too, had flags to wave, for, as June says: 'The Services are part of you and you cannot be bitter or jealous of those wives whose husbands returned. The men went there because there was a job to do and some of them did not come back.' But later, one of the more difficult adjustments to the Servicemen's return to Plymouth was their unavoidable presence on the streets of the city. Sue Enefer knew, even in their civilian clothes, which men were Royal Marines; she has turned away from couples holding hands, and has had to stop herself from asking strangers if they had known her husband.

Both women were anxious to know exactly how their husbands had died. Sue knew there might be some delays, as her husband's unit was based at Arbroath; but, on the return of Andy Evan's 3 Commando Brigade Air Squadron to Plymouth, June went immediately to talk to his major and co-pilot, Sergeant Eddie Candlish. 'I am sure they would have come to me eventually, and perhaps it was a bit unfair going to see Eddie so soon, but I needed to know straightaway.' She was told how, during the San Carlos Bay landings on 21 May, Andy and Eddie were in one of two Gazelle helicopters on escort duty for a Sea King helicopter, which was looking for suitable sites for Rapier missiles. As the aircraft approached Cameron's Point, they were fired upon by Argentine soldiers, despite earlier reports that there were none in the area. Although wounded, Andy managed to ditch his helicopter safely in the sea; Eddie got him into the water before it sank and spent the next twenty minutes struggling to reach the shore, while raked by machine gun fire from the retreating Argentines. The crew of the second helicopter were killed instantly as their Gazelle crashed in flames. Falklands islanders who had seen the incident rushed down to the beach to help Eddie and his fatally wounded colleague ashore, and take them to a nearby farmhouse where Andy died. The next day he was buried at sea from the troopship, *Canberra*. Andy's skill in ditching the helicopter saved his co-pilot's life and had been witnessed by troops already ashore; his bravery earned him a posthumous mention in despatches for distinguished service.

It was June who, at the St Paul's Falklands service on 26 July, introduced Sue to another Royal Marine widow,

Elaine Evans, whom she had known when they were both stationed in Malta with their husbands. Sue discovered that Elaine's husband had also been with 45 Commando and was killed in the same incident as Roger, although it was the first she knew that three other Marines had died at that time. In November that year the two women attended a memorial service together for their men at the squadron's home-base in Arbroath. It was a poignant weekend as, just days before, Roger Enefer's body had been returned to England along with those of sixty-four other servicemen whose families had requested they be brought home for reburial; only twenty-two of those families requested a military funeral. Although Sue had been in touch with her MP and the Royal Marines about her request, no one ever officially notified her that the Prime Minister and the Ministry of Defence, in the face of mounting pressure not only from bereaved families but sections of the Armed Forces, had agreed to the bodies being returned. It was a journalist from a local television studio who rang Sue with the news of their decision.

Weeks passed with no further news, but at the end of October, when Sue read that a container ship was on its way to Southampton with the coffins on board, she phoned the Marines local families' officer in Plymouth and said she wanted to know the arrival date so she could be on the quay when the *Sir Bedivere* docked. She was told the ship would berth in the early hours of the morning and no one, including the families, would be allowed on the dock. She was given the same information when she called the day before the ship's arrival on 16 November and was very upset the following evening when she saw a television news film of families waiting on the dockside as the Union Jack-draped containers holding the coffins were lowered from the ship. 'I wasn't even told when to expect the arrival of Roger's casket in Plymouth. My sister, who was driving home, saw a hearse coming into the city with a casket draped with the Union Jack and just knew it was Roger. Soon after, they called me to discuss the arrangements.' Sue remembers the dignified military funeral the Marines arranged as 'beautiful'; her husband had been killed in May, it was now November, and, despite her grief, she was able to jest with her family that Roger, who had always been so unpunctual, really was late for his own funeral.

'It had taken months to get him back.' The only incident that still annoys her was the loss of Roger's Royal Marine cap, which had originally been returned to her with other personal possessions, and then placed on the casket for the funeral service. The Marines escort party mistakenly took it back to Arbroath and, despite repeated requests, and an attempt to convince her that a different size cap belonged to her husband, it was never returned.

Both Sue and June were touched by the personal concern of individual soldiers who had known their husbands and who visited them on their return to England. In contrast was the insensitive manner in which the bureaucratic Service machine occasionally handled June Evans' bereavement and reduced her to tears and anger. One morning a brown paper parcel arrived in the post; inside a plastic shopping bag from a local Plymouth store was the Union Jack that had covered Sergeant Evans' body before his burial at sea. There was no letter to explain who had sent it or why. Another post brought a photograph taken of her husband's burial service, four bodies in the shrouds used in committals at sea lay on the deck of the *Canberra* draped in Union Jacks. Again, there was no covering letter or indication of who had sent the picture, and one of June's neighbours insisted on taking the photograph away for safe-keeping, anxious not to leave June alone to brood over it. Eight months after Andy died, a warrant officer turned up out of the blue from the Army's distribution depot at Poole with a suitcase of Andy's clothes. June had asked that only his personal belongings be returned and had already received them. To save the officer the trouble of taking them back, she told him to leave them in the garage. It was weeks before she could steel herself to discard the contents, other than a pair of her husband's wellington boots which, for some inexplicable reason, she could not bring herself to part with. The incident that upset her most happened just before Christmas, when an officer called with Andy's South Atlantic campaign medal. It lay in pieces in a brown paper bag; the oakleaf pin to mark his mention in despatches for distinguished service had not even been attached to the ribbon. Sergeant Evans's widow refused to accept it. Three months later at Stonehouse Barracks, Major General Michael Wilkins presented the medal to June and her son, Mark, in a black, felt-lined case with Andy's other service medals, one for duties in Northern Ireland, another for work with the United Nations in Cyprus and a third for his fifteen years' service with the Royal Marines.

The contemptuous manner in which Andy's unassembled medal was originally handed to his widow was not uncommon. Petty Officer Frank Foulkes' posthumous medal arrived in the post in three pieces in a jiffy bag. When his widow, Dorothy, not knowing what it was, tugged the bag open, one of the pieces flew across the room and it took her a week to find it at the bottom of the fruit bowl. She quietly points out that there is a Royal Navy base, HMS *Inskip*, just three miles from their home and an Army camp down the road at Weeton. The local papers were full of photographs of official presentations of campaign medals at both Service bases. 'Don't you think it would have been nice if someone had invited us along to one of those and given us Frank's medal too?'

And when Jason Burt's mother, Theresa, asked if his campaign medal could be laid inside her son's funeral casket at his reburial along with sixteen other soldiers from the Parachute Regiment in Aldershot's military cemetery that November, she was told there had been no time to engrave his name and display it properly. The medal again arrived at his parents' East End London home as it had arrived at Dorothy Foulkes' house, by post in a jiffy bag, and his mother says Jason, who had never won a medal for anything in his brief seventeen years, 'would have been so proud to have worn it had he lived'.

The majority of the parents of the 121 single men, like Jason Burt, who were killed in the Falklands were isolated in their grief, not only from each other but from the Armed Forces in which their sons had given their lives. Their unfamiliarity with the Services made it difficult for them to accept what the Forces regard as routine procedures for dealing with families and bereavement. The occasional dismissive manner in which the Services reacted to requests for details on how their sons had died, or what had happened to personal possessions, reinforced some parents' belief that their sons' lives mattered less than those who had had wives and children.

Theresa and Sidney Burt's eldest son, Jason, was just

sixteen when he joined the Parachute Regiment on 5 September 1980, much against his father's wishes. Sidney Burt is a stallholder in London's famous Petticoat Lane market, and he tore up Jason's original application papers, determined that no son of his 'would die in Northern Ireland'. When it was clear that Jason had inherited his father's stubbornness, and would join the regiment without parental consent at eighteen, Sidney Burt signed the second application, convinced that his five-foot-two skinny son would never survive the Paras' notorious induction course for recruits. On Jason's first weekend home from Tidworth Barracks, the skin peeled off his back where his rucksack had rubbed him raw and his hands were gloved in blisters, but there were no second thoughts. He got his wings on 22 January 1982 and, eleven weeks after his passing-out parade, the now five-foot-nine soldier was despatched to the Falklands, although he was not eligible for service in Northern Ireland until his eighteenth birthday on 28 July.

His battalion were among the first ashore at Port San Carlos on 21 May; their advance on foot across the island to Port Stanley included a twenty-four hour march, exhaustive night engagements with the Argentines, and a forty-eight hour siege of Mount Longdon, under constant mortar and artillery fire, at the beginning of which Sergant Ian McKay and sixteen of his fellow soldiers from 3 Para were killed. The final push to take Mount Longdon was achieved by rifle, grenade and bayonet in hand-to-hand fighting, during which Jason Burt and two of his friends were killed. The three boy soldiers had been junior Paras together. Like Jason, his friend Ian Scrivens was still seventeen; Neil Grose had celebrated his eighteenth birthday on the battlefield the day before.

On Monday, 14 June, the day the war finally ended, two men dressed in civilian clothes approached Sidney Burt as he left the washrooms in Petticoat Market. They told him they were from Chelsea Barracks, that his son had been killed, and handed him a piece of paper with a telephone number which he could ring so someone could visit him and his wife. Jason's father had to be stopped by nearby stallholders from physically attacking the men, who quickly left the market. The telephone number was for the Parachute Regiment's training centre at Tidworth Barracks, but, despite repeated calls, no one came to see the Burts until Wednesday morning. It was one of the men from Chelsea Barracks, this time in a Para uniform, and Theresa insisted she be told how her son had died: 'The papers had said they were fighting hand-to-hand with bayonets and I was going mad imagining all sorts of things. I wanted to know if he was injured, how long he had lived and how exactly did he die. But the man kept saying they did not give minor details like that.' Her grief erupted in anger when that week a local paper contacted her to ask how old Jason was, as the Ministry of Defence had refused to confirm there were any seventeen-year-old soldiers in the Falklands. She offered them Jason's birth certificate as proof.

The parents of Jason Burt immediately requested that he be brought home for reburial, even if they had to make private arrangements and pay for it themselves. His younger brother, Jarvis, wrote to Prince Charles, the Parachute Regiment's Colonel in Chief, and received a personally signed letter which told him, while it was the Paras' tradition to lie where they had fallen, the government was considering individual requests, and the Prince would inform the Ministry of Defence of Jarvis' letter. Theresa appealed as a mother to Margaret Thatcher, telling her in a letter how she had seen her crying on television when her son Mark was lost in the Sahara desert: 'So surely she would understand why I wanted my son's body brought home. I got a formal acknowledgement saying the matter was being considered.'

The public announcement that the Falklands casualties would be brought back for reburial brought a swift offer from a representative from the British Legion who knocked on the Burts' front door the same evening. She said she had just received a telephone call from her branch secretary telling her to come round and see them 'before the Chingford crowd can reach you'. As Jason was a local boy, they would like to offer his family the use of their British Legion flag for his coffin during the funeral. This was the first time the British Legion had contacted them. Jason Burt's parents were as upset that the Legion should have taken such an initiative at such a time as they had been at the attitude of the official from the Services charity, SSAFA, who visited them a few weeks after their son's death and advised them to pull themselves together and be proud of how their son had died. Theresa remembers how the man, who had lost a leg in the First World War, was silenced by her reply that she did not need her son to die to feel proud of him.

The Burts eventually pieced together their son's last hours from the accounts of Jason's fellow soldiers, who visited them on their return, but the fact that they were never officially told still angers his mother. The answer she really seeks and will never be given is why soldiers under eighteen, who are not eligible to die on the streets of Northern Ireland, should have been allowed to die in the Falklands. Perhaps it would have been better for Theresa never to have known the circumstances of her son's death, but her knowledge of his last days strengthens her resolve to pursue her claim for Jason's Army insurance, which, after five inquiries, the Ministry of Defence still insist Jason never signed for.

Young Jason Burt went to war wearing his mother's wedding ring because he felt in need of luck; the ring was never returned. Jason never swore in front of his mother, but in his last letter home he cursed his feet, as he had trench foot, and was trying to take his mind off the discomfort by guessing what the family might be preparing for his birthday. Jason's fellow soldiers told his mother how her son's feet were so bad the only alternative was to leave him behind to freeze, or keep him moving, in the hope the next time casualties were lifted out of the area by helicopter Jason would be taken off the battlefield. They recalled that after forty-eight hours, during which they had eaten only dehydrated food and had run out of water, Jason and his friend had tried to melt two Mars Bars with a box of matches into their porridge oats. Knowing these things, and the final act of violence that killed her son, will remain with his mother for ever, and the visit from the 3rd Paras Lieutenant Colonel Hew Pike and padre Derek Heaver, who spoke of their respect as veterans for the bravery of a boy soldier, will never diminish her belief that her son should not have been there in the first place.

When Don and Marion Pryce's only son, Donald, a twenty-six-year-old aircraft electrical mechanic in the Fleet Air Arm, died on the *Atlantic Conveyor* on 25 May, his parents received VIP treatment from Naval personnel, compared with the experience of Cunard widow, Dorothy Foulkes, whose husband Frank was one of the twelve casualties. Don Pryce is quick to point out that, as he works as a technical officer at Fleetlands, the Royal Navy's aircraft maintenance base near his Fareham home, and his wife Marion is a clerical assistant secretary employed by the Ministry of Defence at HMS *Centurion*, Gosport, it would have been difficult for the authorities to have missed them. Rear Admiral Simpson of HMS *Nelson*, Portsmouth, immediately telephoned them personally to see if there was anything he could do, a captain called at their home with a navigation chart to show them the exact spot where Donald had been buried at sea, and a Royal Navy staff car with a Lieutenant as chauffeur and a Petty Officer escort, both of them recently returned from their secondment to the *Atlantic Conveyor*, were detailed to drive them to and from the memorial service for the ship in its home port of Liverpool. Ironically, Don Pryce had spent two years in the Falklands in 1966–68 on the patrol ship, the HMS *Protector*, as part of his twenty-seven years' service with the Fleet Air Arm. In the family's front garden at Fareham is a large, smooth, whale bone his son Donald had asked his father to bring back from the South Atlantic as a souvenir. Don Pryce senior was the chief artificer for 891 Squadron when he first met a newly qualified naval pilot, Michael Layard, later the RN Captain posted to the *Conveyor* to work with Cunard's Captain Ian North. Poignantly they met again at the Liverpool memorial service, and the Pryces told him how shocked they had been to discover their son was aboard the *Conveyor*. They thought he was working on the aircraft carrier, HMS *Invincible*, servicing the Wessex helicopters.

Marion Pryce's work at HMS *Centurion* in the release office included arranging the discharge papers of naval personnel who had left or died in Service. Later that year, despite an offer from a colleague to process her son's papers, she insisted on handling the formalities herself, discharging her son as deceased from 845 Squadron Fleet Air Arm. When the office staff were asked to compile address lists for the South Atlantic campaign medals, she quietly arranged that her son's medal, and that of another young bachelor casualty from the same base, be officially presented to the two families when they visited the squadron at Yeovilton.

No matter how considerate the behaviour of certain Naval staff, nothing will ever make up for what the Pryce family feel is their very shabby treatment by the trustees of the South Atlantic Fund who, they believe, have valued the life of their son and that of other single men much lower than those who were married, by the way they have distributed the public's £16 million. It is a feeling common to the sixty parents of single men killed in the Falklands, who have formed a pressure group to lobby for a fairer share of the remaining money. A potent part of their anger is the conviction of parents, like Don and Marion Pryce, the Stockwells and the Burts, that the Falklands was not worth the loss of one Argentine or British life.

The brevity of the war, the rapid shift in public and government interest once the war was over, has made it difficult for them and many widows not to feel they have been forgotten with indecent haste. The war was bitterly brief; just seventy-four days after the Falkland Islands were invaded, Major General Jeremy Moore accepted the Argentines' surrender from Major General Mario Menendez in Port Stanley. There seemed little time for grief as the newspapers and television coverage switched to events on their own doorstep: the first glimpse of a new-born prince and future king; an intruder in the Queen's bedroom at Buckingham Palace; and, even before the Falklands memorial service at St Paul's on 26 July, the horror of the Hyde Park and Regent's Park IRA bombs, in which eleven soldiers died and a shrapnel-scarred horse called Sefton became a national hero destined to receive more public affection and attention than any one of the soldiers injured in the Falklands.

The need of the fully stretched Armed Forces to return as quickly as possible to their normal routine, which had been so rudely and unpredictably interrupted by a military dictator in the South Atlantic, left those whose lives had been irrevocably turned upside down confused and angry. Women would soon discover they had no role in the Services in which their husbands had given their lives, not that their part was ever more than a social one when the men were alive. Maureen Emly momentarily escaped with her sister Pat and son Matthew to the fantasy world of Walt Disney in America's

Orlando. Anita Flanagan and Dorothy Foulkes busied themselves in the way they had always found most rewarding, creating a home for their children, this time homes of their own instead of a married quarter or a council house. Marica McKay found herself compulsively shopping every day the first month after Ian's death; she returned with her sister to Bahrain for a holiday, only to go back restlessly to Aldershot after ten days because she did not like the heat.

A couple of months after the death of her able seaman husband Stephen Heyes on HMS *Ardent*, his twenty-two-year-old widow, Christina, went to her local post office to collect her war widow's pension; as a childless woman under forty she was entitled to £8.88 a week. She got a puzzled look from the cashier, and an inquisitive elderly woman in the queue behind her demanded: 'What war?'

CHAPTER FOUR:

The war-wounded return home

'He was one of Margaret Thatcher's "boys", a hero, but when it was over nobody wanted to know.' Tina Brookes, wife of an injured paratrooper.

The mid-morning arrival of the VC-10 at RAF Brize Norton, Oxon, on 13 July 1982 was a quiet affair. There were no military bands or bunting, none of the public razzamatazz of a heroes' welcome for the task force soldiers who disembarked from the twenty-hour flight from Montevideo. Some of the men were sedated, carefully strapped on stretchers that were lifted gently into waiting ambulances. Other soldiers, like Royal Engineer Corporal 'Baz' Morgan, whose right foot was blown off by an Argentine mine near Port Stanley insisted on painfully making their own way on crutches to the buses that sped them through the English countryside to Wroughton RAF hospital and their anxious, assembled families. Corporal Morgan remembers that some of the injured 'were not a pretty sight, not the sort of picture to put on a television screen or in a newspaper'.

Their low key return from the Falklands was to set the tone for the Ministry of Defence's handling of anything to do with the war's casualties. Just as the Ministry was at first adamant that none of the bodies of men killed in the South Atlantic war would be returned for re-burial in Britain, they were equally determined that the injured Servicemen would not detract from their triumphal propaganda. They remained silent when London's Lord Mayor initially banned injured soldiers from taking part in his victory parade through the City, an event hosted in presidential style by the Prime Minister, Margaret Thatcher, rather than a member of the Royal Family or Armed Services.

Once home with their families or in military hospitals, the Falkland casualties were too worried about the future or too ill to do anything other than trust that their affairs would be handled compassionately by the authorities. Some officers who had fought beside their injured men gave much needed moral support to the soldiers and their families but they were powerless when it came to dealing with penal and petty Service regulations, like the stoppage of various allowances for the medically unfit or the silence in Whitehall about payments to the injured from the publicly subscribed South Atlantic Fund. When Major Roger Patton, second in command of the 3rd Battalion Parachute Regiment, publicly criticised the running of the Fund which, three months after their return, had done nothing for the injured soldiers in his regiment, the Defence Ministry made it clear that his outburst was a serious breach of etiquette. When the same Ministry refused to give details of casualties to established organisations like the British Limbless Ex-Service Men's Association, BLESMA, whose expertise in counselling and practical advice is valued by thousands of disabled Servicemen, individual regimental officers just quietly passed on the information themselves without Ministerial clearance.

The overwhelming impression among the families of the injured was the sooner the men returned to normal duties or left the Services the better. A disabled soldier is of little use to a fighting force honed to peak physical fitness. What sort of future could the Services offer a paratrooper with one leg who could no longer do the only job he was trained for? When the men themselves started to ask such questions there was an embarrassed silence. If the Services were not geared to cope with the continued presence of the war's casualties, they were even less clued up on how to handle families trying to adjust to the situation. A common response was to ignore problems or deny their existence. The classic panacea was a visit from Army doctors to the wives of Welsh Guards at Pirbright to offer sleeping tablets or tranquillisers. Equally insulting was the flying inspection by a voluntary worker from an Army Service charity to the home of a severely wounded Scots

75

Guardsman. As the visitor pried into the contents of the kitchen fridge, she made it quite clear that she was interested only in the possible neglect of the Guardsman's children, rather than the distress of his wife, angry with the authorities for not telling her or her husband what their future might be. Visits like these were worse than being totally ignored, as they reinforced the feeling that nobody really knew what to do. One wife concluded: 'The Army's attitude was that we knew what we were getting into when we married and that it was up to us to sort something out, preferably as far away as possible from the regiment.'

Few of the wives had believed when the task force set sail that their men would 'do battle', never mind be killed or injured. The families of the Scots Guards thought their men had been earmarked to garrison the islands once the Argentines had fled before the threat of the advancing task force, or withdrawn through a negotiated settlement. Many families of Welsh Guardsmen believed their men would never get as far as the Falklands but would turn round for home at Ascension Island, the threat of Britain's armada having done the trick and put the invaders to flight. No one attempted to correct these assumptions. It is therefore not surprising that families were as unprepared to deal with the aftermath of the war as the bloody realities of the battles that flashed across their television screens. As the casualty figures rose, the credibility gap between what they had been allowed to believe might happen and the lists of dead and injured Servicemen only increased their apprehension of what to expect when the men returned home.

In Britain, the Bluff Cove disaster required the sort of response expected of a civil authority in the event of a major air crash or mining tragedy. In the close-knit communities of Wales practically every family knew or was related to someone who was, or had been, in the Welsh Guards and the bombing of the *Sir Galahad* and *Sir Tristram* touched many lives. For the Welsh, with thirty-eight Guardsmen dead and eighty-five wounded, some of them horribly burnt, Bluff Cove was equivalent to a national disaster and should never have been left just to the military and voluntary organisations to handle unsupervised. In many cases the military's inability to deal sensitively, never mind efficiently, with the situation only compounded the distress of families frantic for news of their husbands and sons.

Simon Weston was the most badly injured Guardsman to survive Bluff Cove; he had forty-six per cent burns to his hands, face and body. Taken ashore from the still smouldering *Sir Galahad*, he was not transferred to the hospital ship *Uganda*, but left at Ajax Bay, where a medical orderly was detailed to make him comfortable as he was not expected to live. On 9 June at Simon's home in Nelson, mid-Glamorgan, his mother, Pauline Hatfield, who had remarried when Simon and his sister were children, watched the ITV 5.45 news headlines. Pauline says she will never forget reporter Michael Nicholson's voice describing the ship's life-rafts disintegrating as they dropped from the deck of the *Sir Galahad* into a sea of burning oil. The precise timetable of telephone calls, distress and confusion that followed will also remain with her for the rest of her life.

At 10.40 pm that evening the telephone interrupted ITN's *News At Ten*. It was a call from the London headquarters of the Welsh Guards at Wellington Barracks to say Simon had been injured but not seriously. The caller gave Mrs Hatfield a number to phone for further information and asked where she would be during the next twenty-four hours. At 7 pm on 11 June, a sergeant phoned from Wellington Barracks to say Simon had four per cent burns, it was not serious and they did not know if the injuries were to his hands or face. At 8.45 pm on 13 June a Welsh Guards liaison officer came to the Hatfield house to tell them Simon had forty-six per cent burns but the extent and degree of his injuries were not known. As a district nurse, Pauline Hatfield was only too aware of the seriousness of such injuries and was very distressed. After two mistaken reports in four days she did not know what to believe and when she asked how Simon was the liaison officer told her he was 'very seriously ill, critical'. She pressed him as to what he meant and he replied, 'critical and dying'. She remembers saying: ' "I didn't want to see you," meaning the longer he had stayed away from us the better the news of Simon would have been. Instead, he thought it was a personal insult and he never came again, never at all. That was the liaison officer from the Welsh Guards.'

For several days there was no further news, although the family phoned everyone they could think of. Pauline's second husband is a quiet, gentle Yorkshireman more than twenty years her senior and a retired hospital engineer. He is slow to anger and not one to make a fuss. Early on the morning of Ladies' Day at Ascot, he phoned Wellington Barracks and said if he did not get any news of Simon by 1 o'clock he would send a telegram to Prince Charles, the Welsh Guards' Colonel-in-Chief, asking for his help. At 12.53 pm a Warrant Officer phoned him to say: 'I have beaten you by seven minutes, Mr Hatfield. Simon is no longer on the very seriously ill list and, although he is still serious, he is improving.' That weekend the Hatfield family were told Simon had been taken by the hospital ship *Hydra* to Montevideo and was being flown home to RAF Brize Norton. The Hatfields drove to the airport to meet the flight number they had been given. Simon was not on the plane. The RAF showed them a passenger list where Simon's name had been deleted and a Jennings substituted. The RAF personnel were very kind; they took the family to a nearby hotel for a meal while they made inquiries and a Wing Commander personally came and explained that the pilot on Simon's flight had thought him too ill to travel and would not take the responsibility of bringing him home on a twenty-hour journey. On Friday the Hatfields telephoned Wellington Barracks to see if Simon had been allocated another weekend flight. Whoever answered the phone told them that all the Welsh Guards had gone home for the weekend, that Simon's whereabouts had nothing to do with him, and that they should call again on Monday.

Pauline Hatfield spent the weekend curled up in a sitting room chair, rocking herself backwards and forwards; she also lost her voice. She is an energetic forty-two-year-old who rarely lets anything get on top of her – an intelligent, caring and much valued district nurse, whose duties include the domiciliary care of psychiatric patients living with their families. Fifteen months after Simon's homecoming, her voice still falls to a whisper when she remembers: 'That weekend I was like a psychotic. They had lifted me up and put me down. First he was injured, but not seriously, then he was serious, then critical and dying – and then nothing.'

On Monday, anger spurred her to call Maindy Barracks

and demand to know where her son was and when he was coming home. She was told that Simon would be arriving on the 6.20 am flight on Wednesday 30 June. Simon was not on that flight, nor the second one. The Hatfields and Pauline's parents got back in their car and drove straight to Maindy Barracks and asked to see the liaison officer. The duty sergeant, aware of their distress, said: 'Come on, my shoulders are broad enough, throw it at me.' Pauline asked where Simon was: 'I remember this tall, handsome regimental sergeant major who was passing bending over from his great height and saying, "You do realise he is being well taken care of." My mammy nearly broke her knuckles hitting the filing cabinet and told him, "You do realise he is a human being and not a piece of wood you are talking about, and he is very precious to us and we want to know where he is." ' It was the RAF who found out when Simon was coming home by telephoning the Royal Navy in Portsmouth for details of the injured still on the hospital ships. They were told Simon was scheduled for transfer to a flight arriving at 6.20 am on 2 July. Pauline Hatfield told me that nothing in her life has been so devastating as those twenty-four desperate days from the time they told her Simon was injured to the day he returned: 'Nothing could ever again hurt me so utterly.'

It is difficult to find excuses for such prolonged confusion by the Welsh Guards. The RAF could provide positive information, why did the Welsh Guards not use similar channels? Why was no one at their headquarters at Wellington Barracks detailed to remain on twenty-four hour standby, including weekends, to answer any queries from families about injured Guardsmen, until all had returned to England and their relatives knew exactly where they were? Simon Weston's family were not the only ones who, having been told their men were injured, were not kept fully informed by their battalion headquarters on their condition, their whereabouts or when they would be coming home. The Bluff Cove disaster was on 8 June; seven days later the war had ended and, with the cessation of hostilities, there was no strategic reason for limiting communications with the South Atlantic: the wounded were even allowed to telephone home from the hospital ships.

Some families only discovered the extent of their men's

injuries when the men themselves phoned or sent telegrams. The wife of a Scots Guardsman, on being told her husband had had 'an accident' and broken his arm, thought: 'Typical, he has tripped over his big feet again. It was only when I got a telegram from him saying he was wounded that I realised he had been shot.' The medical care of the war's casualties cannot be faulted: shattered limbs were saved that in earlier military engagements would have been amputated, the nursing care of the critical burns cases was such that everyone who reached the hospital ships survived. But what of the care of the families who waited at home? When a Guardsman's wife insisted the families' officer give her the details of her husband's amputation, he handed over the report for her to read herself. 'He was choked, he had just told four women they were widows and there was me frantic about my husband losing a limb. It is dreadful to have a husband killed in a war but all I cared about at that time was my man, while everyone was paying more attention to the families of the dead than the living.'

When Tina Brookes, who was living with her parents in Sheffield, phoned the 2nd Battalion Parachute Regiment in Aldershot for news of her wounded husband, Leslie, the families' officer was more concerned that she was not living locally in married quarters and told her that had she been in the neighbourhood she could have come into the barracks to read the bulletins. It was Leslie's call from the hospital ship *Uganda* to Tina, whom he had married five weeks before going to the Falklands, that told her he would be home on 26 June. Royal Marine Christopher White actually phoned his wife, Gillian, from RAF Wroughton to say he had arrived and why was there no one there to meet him? The day before, Gillian's sister-in-law had seen Chris on a television news clip boarding a VC-10 transport plane at Montevideo; but when Gillian telephoned the Royal Marines barracks in Plymouth, the welfare officer could not confirm that Chris was coming home. Marine Kevin Woodford, a twenty-two-year-old who had lost a leg during the *Sir Galahad* bombing, could not wait to get back to England and he remembers thinking as he arrived at Wroughton that at last he would see his mum and dad, and maybe his girlfriend, but there was no one there. It was not until the next day, when he was transferred to Haslar, the

Royal Navy's hospital in Gosport, that his family in Keyworth, Notts, knew he was back home.

There was a time-lag of up to three weeks between the date when the war's casualties were first hospitalised and their arrival back in England, and during that time no one from the medical or welfare side of the Services appears to have helped prepare the families for coping with their husbands' or sons' injuries. No one knew how a man looked after being disfigured by an exploding Exocet missile, no one could imagine the state of mind of a young sports-mad soldier who had lost a leg, or the apprehension of a newly married Guardsman about how his bride would view his charred body.

There had been so many confused reports about the degree and extent of injuries that both the wounded and their waiting families did not know how it would be meeting each other for the first time. At Wroughton and the Queen Elizabeth Military Hospital, Woolwich, where the burns cases were taken to a specially prepared unit, there was no one at hand, other than Service padres and Red Cross volunteers, to help counsel relatives. Therapists trained in crisis intervention might have been able to help some of them through the initial shock and distress at the men's injuries.

It is appalling that a system that could so rapidly mobilise a twenty-eight thousand strong task force was so incapable of dealing with the consequences of such a brief, bitter war. The casualty figures had been mercifully low – in many instances, as a result of the skills of on-the-spot medical teams – 255 dead, 777 injured, of which 365 were moderately to severely wounded, including 30 men who had lost limbs and 120 burns cases. At a time when the families of the war's casualties desperately needed information and advice, there was none. At a time when the injured wanted some idea about their future, none was given. A soldier who lost a leg in the battle for Mount Longdon told me: 'The biggest thing about getting better is reassurance. What the nurses on the ship couldn't tell us was how it was going to be for the wife and kids when we got home, and what about the future? It is worries like that which keep you awake at night, as well as the physical pain.'

What of the care of those families who, eighteen months later, still nursed their wounded? Pauline Hatfield's assessment of her experience summarises the feelings of many: 'I know there are all types of people who make up a community, but if only someone had come to see us, had bothered to find out what sort of family we are, had cared enough to see we are intelligent, sensible people who can handle whatever they have to tell us. But nobody came, either then or later, or even now. The post-care of the families is shocking.'

Private Leslie Brookes of A Company 2nd Battalion Parachute Regiment was a veteran of the battles of Darwin and Goose Green, where his commander, Lt Col 'H' Jones, and sixteen other soldiers were killed. He was shot in the mouth on 13 June at Wireless Ridge during the final push for Port Stanley. Within the next twenty-four hours, soldiers from 2 Para were the first British troops to enter the town since the Argentine occupation eleven weeks before. Leslie was taken by helicopter to the *Uganda*; he had lost teeth and gums on the left side of his mouth, an injury that required painful and complicated dental surgery and has left a permanent facial scar. His mother, Lilian, the warden of a pensioners' housing scheme in Sheffield, remembers that the families who went to Brize Norton to meet the wounded were not allowed into the airport, where the planes landed on the far side of a runway so that no one could see the casualties being transferred by ambulance and bus. As the men arrived at RAF Wroughton hospital, Lilian says: 'A lot of wives and mothers were dreadfully upset. One wife was breaking her heart because her husband refused to let her see him, he was obviously so badly injured he did not know how she would take it.' Leslie's parents and wife praised the Red Cross, who could not do enough for the families and kept them supplied with endless cups of tea and sandwiches. But the volunteers, too, were often overwhelmed by the distress around them; there had been nothing comparable since the Second World War and, despite their training, few had personal experience of handling such situations.

Joan M* had been told her Welsh Guardsman husband had survived the Bluff Cove disaster with two per cent burns to his

---

* Joan, like many Servicemen's wives I spoke to, did not want to be identified as her husband is still in the Services and families are not supposed to give interviews without authorisation.

body. She assumed that three weeks' medical treatment on the *Uganda* would have left him well enough to convalesce at home on his return to England. When she went with other families from the Welsh Guards Pirbright barracks to meet the returning casualties, she took a change of clothes for her husband to travel home in. When the men had been temporarily settled into a ward, their relatives were ushered in for a strictly timed visit. Joan M knew without having to ask the doctors that her husband would not be going home with her that day. He was bandaged from the waist down, the back of his head was one big scab, and all he wanted to know was which of his men had been killed. Mrs M remembers: 'I've seen some unpleasant injuries and I was in the Caterham pub bombing when friends of ours were blown to bits. But I saw things at that hospital I shall never forget for the rest of my life, and no one had prepared us for that. It was particularly cruel to the very young wives and the mothers who were distraught to see their sons, some little more than boys, in such a state.'

Pauline Hatfield, her husband and parents insisted on meeting Simon's flight and the RAF, knowing what the family had been through, allowed them into the airport. They did not recognise Simon as he was lifted from the plane on a stretcher, his body wrapped in foam rubber from head to toe with just a blackened face showing. Simon's gran said, 'Look at that poor boy' and Simon, recognising her voice, called out, 'Mam.' His mother nearly fainted. The Hatfields had assumed, and certainly no one had told them otherwise, that Simon would stay at RAF Wroughton hospital, but within hours of his arrival they were informed Simon was being transferred with the other burns cases by helicopter to the Queen Elizabeth Military Hospital, Woolwich. They later learned that a BBC TV documentary team had arranged with the Woolwich hospital and the Ministry of Defence to film the medical treatment of burns cases from the *Sir Galahad* and, three weeks before his return, the TV film crew had been told that a special room had been prepared in the hospital burns unit for the most critical patient – Simon Weston.

The TV team were waiting at Woolwich that day to film his arrival. The Hatfield family got back in their car and drove to London.

Andrew Wallis, nineteen, of the 36 Royal Engineers, had been attached to the Welsh Guards. Andrew was with two friends on the tank deck of the *Sir Galahad* when it was bombed. One died instantly; Andrew used his bare hands to put out the flames consuming his other friend's clothes. Andrew is Mrs Mara Dawkins' youngest son by her first marriage and she remembers it was a beautiful summer morning when the sergeant major from the Royal Engineers Maidstone barracks came to tell her about her son's injuries. 'He was a very nice bloke who was nervous about getting out of his car because of our dogs. I stood there in the garden and we talked about Andrew as though we were passing the time of day. It just didn't seem possible that such a thing could have happened to him. It was a beautiful English summer morning and my son had been badly injured by a missile and was on a ship the other side of the world. The sergeant major said it was twenty-six per cent burns, but not serious. It wasn't until he came home three weeks later with his hands still wrapped in plastic bags that we knew how awful it was.' Mara and her husband James were about to set out for RAF Wroughton when they were told that Andrew was being transferred to the Woolwich hospital. Eighteen months later the shock of the first meeting still reduced Mrs Dawkins and Andrew's wife, Ann, who was then his girlfriend, to tears. Ann had been out shopping with a girlfriend when the *Sir Galahad* was bombed. She remembered that for no reason at all her stomach 'did a flip' and she told her girlfriend, 'something has happened to Andrew'. Two days later a dozen red roses arrived for her birthday. Andrew had ordered them as a surprise for her before leaving for the Falklands. When Ann was told he was injured, one of her first reactions was to bake him a cake for his twentieth birthday on 11 July. She told me: 'I made this super cake but I could not stop crying, as no one would tell me what his injuries were. I did not know if he had lost his arms, or legs, or what.'

Andrew's stepfather, James, could not wait until the casualties brought by helicopter from Wroughton were taken into the hospital; he ran out in the rain when he heard the Chinook coming down to land. When he returned, his shirt sticking to him from the downpour, all he could say was something about plastic bags on Andrew's hands. Ann was distressed because she could not kiss him: 'His face was like a crisp.' There was no one at the hospital that day who could tell them what they desperately wanted to know – how long it would take Andrew to recover from his injuries and what would he eventually look like? Soon after his return, Mrs Dawkins was at the hospital when some of the Second World War veterans from the Guinea Pig Club came to show the young soldiers burned in the Falklands how successful plastic surgery had been for them and how they could manage without all their fingers. Mara says: 'I know they only meant good, and they really did cheer up some of the lads, but when I saw how unnatural one of them still looked after all that surgery I went back to my car and just sat and cried.'

Gillian White had no idea what to expect of her husband, Chris, of the 1st Raiding Squadron Royal Marines, who had also been on the *Sir Galahad* on 8 June. Originally his family were told he was not injured, but a couple of hours later the welfare officer from the Marines Plymouth barracks phoned again to say he was hurt but was one of the 'walking wounded'. On 10 June, Gillian got another telephone call at their home in Weston-super-Mare. The welfare officer tried to explain that Chris was not physically hurt, but suffering from 'shellshock', or what the doctors sometimes call acute battle reaction, and when he got home she would find him very different for a while. She was left upset and frightened. Chris's father, who had spent twenty-two years in the Royal Navy, knew the textbook definitions but had no experience of Servicemen with shellshock and was as worried as Gillian about his son's condition.

Chris did phone home from the *Uganda* briefly to tell his wife not to worry, and he was looking forward to coming back and being with their three-year-old son, Daniel. Gillian thought it did not sound at all like him and she rang his father in tears, convinced Chris and the Marines were hiding something from her and that he had been horribly wounded. There was no further information on Chris until he returned unannounced at Wroughton hospital and phoned home.

When Gillian and her father-in-law arrived in a rush at the hospital, a staff nurse asked them to wait for someone to brief them about his condition – by now Gillian's imagination was running riot. A male nurse explained that Chris would seem strange as he was taking drugs and had not slept for some time. He took them to a single room at the end of a quiet corridor; the room was in semi-darkness with the curtains half-drawn. Gillian says: 'Chris looked really ill, his eyes were dreadful and he had a piece of paper strung round his neck.' The piece of paper was a white cardboard passenger's landing pass from SS *Uganda*, printed in English and Spanish. On the back was Chris's Service number, PO32334N, and the handwritten diagnosis: '7 days post injury, walking, battle shock, will not communicate verbally with anyone, refuses oral therapy.' During those seven days the only person Chris had spoken to was his wife, when he had telephoned her from the *Uganda*. All Chris can remember of that first meeting in the semi-darkness of the hospital room was 'feeling remarkably cheerful and randy and wanting to go home'.

Not only was he not allowed home, but Gillian was told that, as a Royal Marine, he would be transferred to the Royal Navy hospital in Plymouth, which was near the headquarters of his returning squadron. It was also twice the distance from their home, over two hours drive, while Gillian could get to Wroughton within the hour. She had recently begun work as a laboratory technician for the World Health Organisation tsetse fly research project at Bristol University. It was her first job since having Daniel and she not only enjoyed it but needed the money to help pay the mortgage on the home she had moved to from a council house, while Chris was in the Falklands. She did not want to lose the job, nor did she intend missing a day visiting Chris. The RAF staff doctor she spoke to at Wroughton was quite happy for her husband to stay there in his own room within visiting distance of his family. He stressed how important it was for them to spend as much time as possible with him, but there was little he could do about the Royal Navy's insistence that Marine White was their patient.

There was no one at the hospital that Gillian could discuss the situation with. The only people she knew from Chris's squadron were still in the Falklands; apart from social occasions at her husband's Plymouth barracks, she rarely visited him there, preferring to make their home in Weston-super-Mare where both their families lived. After their wedding they had lived in married quarters in Gosport, but

Gillian disliked the flat, found the area depressing and run-down and, when she was two months pregnant, returned to Weston to live with her parents until they were allocated a council house. Chris was all in favour of the arrangement, even though it meant commuting at weekends. He did not want his son to have the same rootless childhood he had experienced; because of his father's different postings with the Royal Navy, he had been sent to a boarding school when he was twelve and joined the Royal Marines at sixteen. He was thinking of leaving the Marines for the police force in the summer of 1983, when he would have completed ten years' service, and, with Gillian returning to work, they had decided to buy a house in Weston.

Individual domestic arrangements and future plans do not always fit into the military scheme of things, whose priority is the cohesiveness of the Armed Forces – all men wear the same uniform, have the same haircut, live by the same rulebook. The military preference is for families to fall in with their concept of Service life as a self-sufficient, enclosed society with its own welfare, social, medical and educational systems. Too much independence impairs cohesion and efficiency in enforc-ing the rules. The initiative Marine White's family took about his hospitalisation was, therefore, not at all popular in some circles. That weekend they tracked down the secretary of their local MP, Jerry Wiggin, Under Secretary of State at the Ministry of Defence, and asked that Chris be allowed to stay at Wroughton. Mr Wiggins' staff telephoned John Nott's office and inquiries were made in Plymouth. The compromise appears to have been that Chris would complete his current treatment at Plymouth, but should he need future care it would be arranged locally. When he arrived at the Plymouth hospital after an early Monday morning transfer from Wroughton, it was soon made clear to him that no one approved of the family talking to their MP. Chris remembers that, on top of that, he complained bitterly to everyone who would listen that he was going to the newspapers about the *Sir Galahad*: 'To tell them it had been murder leaving the men on those ships without any air cover. It was little wonder they thought me bonkers.'

Gillian could get to Plymouth by late afternoon if she started work at six in the morning, left at 2 pm to collect

Daniel and arranged a lift with family or friends, because she did not trust her old Anglia to make the round trip without breaking down. On her first visit she was summoned to a side office to meet one of her husband's doctors. She recalls him saying had she not been a 'bit silly' going to their MP, and that such a move had been quite unnecessary as they were the ones qualified to make the best decision for Chris. After all, it was not their fault that she had travel problems when she could be living locally in married quarters like other soldiers' wives. Gillian tried to explain that she had approached their MP because there was no one else she could turn to, and she felt the family should be allowed to have some say where Chris was hospitalised. It would also be easier for the whole family and their son Daniel – not just for her – if Chris were nearer home, as she particularly wanted Daniel to spend as much time as possible with his father in the hope it might motivate and stabilise him. 'When he realised that I was prepared to argue, and not call him "sir", his whole attitude changed. After that it was more or less "OK, just get on with it."' Chris was allowed home the following weekend and, for the first time since leaving the *Sir Galahad*, he slept naturally. He returned to Plymouth for an assessment, was given a series of out-patient appointments with a psychiatrist at the hospital, and went back to his family in Weston for an extended sick-leave.

The role of the family in the care of the sick has become standard medical practice in many hospitals, where visiting hours are flexible and relatives are encouraged to participate in non-specialist nursing care, such as helping a patient take a bath. The presence of a caring relative rooting for the patient's recovery can be as beneficial as any pill. The young men who had returned shocked and injured from the Falklands needed their families, and the staff at the Queen Elizabeth Military Hospital, Woolwich, encouraged relatives to spend as much time as possible with them. The Army's Wellington and Chelsea Barracks in London and Pirbright camp laid on transport to take families living in married quarters to the hospital. But the average age of the task force soldier was nineteen and many of the injured were single men whose families lived all over Britain. Soon after they returned there was a national rail strike and, if families did not have their own transport or could arrange for someone to give them a lift, they could not visit their sons, while those who came from some distance had to find accommodation. There were many families who just could not afford to visit as often as they would have liked. Service charities like the Soldiers' Sailors' and Airmen's Families Association, SSAFA, usually make it their business to cover expenses in these circumstances, but in the time-honoured traditions of Britain's outdated Victorian charity laws, recipients not only have first to ask, but also prove need. In a Welfare State like Britain the concept of 'poor laws' no longer exists; people are entitled to financial provision and benefits from the State; if they are in need it is their right to receive help and anathema to a post-Bevanite generation to seek monies from a charity. Even when families were aware that the numerous Armed Forces charities might cover the sort of circumstances they found themselves in, and few had heard about organisations like SSAFA, no one knew how to approach them, and certainly did not want to appear to be 'begging'.

The aftermath of the Falklands War desperately required an instant and flexible response to the families of the injured who might have some financial problems; the onus was on the charities to take the initiative. Rarely did they do so. Their national headquarters are run almost exclusively by a generation of retired senior-ranking Armed Forces personnel who duplicate the attitudes of the most conformist sections of the military hierarchy, believing that everything should be handled strictly by the rulebook, in this case, sticking to the letter of the charity laws. It was this blinkered interpretation of the outdated British charity laws that caused so much upset and bitterness when it came to administrating the South Atlantic Fund.

Some regimental welfare officers did take the step before the rail strike of sending travel warrants to families living some distance from hospitals. These and petrol expenses were paid for from regimental funds and eventually reimbursed from the £16 million publicly subscribed South Atlantic Fund. But there was no attempt to set up a comprehensive scheme whereby families of the injured would automatically have their travel and accommodation arranged and paid for, without having to ask each time they wanted to visit the injured men. It is shocking that some soldiers who were, and still are, long-term patients were not given every possible help for their families to visit and stay near them. Where cases were known personally to officers who had fought alongside their injured men, they made sure every help was given to them and their families, but many of the wounded were separated from their battalions, who were still in the Falklands or based some distance from the military hospitals, and within a year of the war some battalions went abroad on extended training sessions to Norway and Canada or overseas tours to Belize.

When the Hatfield family arrived at Woolwich hospital the day Simon returned home, it was the hospital staff who eventually arranged accommodation for them for two nights and for Pauline to stay as a paying guest for the three weeks Simon was on the critical list.

Mrs Dawkins, who was at the hospital that day to see her son Andrew, remembers some of the families had travelled from Wales and the Midlands, not knowing where they were going to spend the night, and her sister-in-law offered to put one couple up. The military hospitals were flooded with gifts for the returning injured soldiers. Marks & Spencer sent toilet soap and flannels, local businessmen delivered alcohol, cigarettes and chocolates, the Queen sent flowers and ladies from the London Welsh society baked Welsh cakes for the Welsh Guards; show business stars and beauty queens queued to visit, so did members of the Royal Family and a pool of volunteers from the respective Friends of the Hospital. But families like the Hatfields and the Dawkins, who spent as much time as possible at the Woolwich, can remember some soldiers who hardly saw their relatives after the first homecoming visit because of the expense and distance they had to travel.

The families of the injured soldiers have nothing but praise for the surgical skills of the doctors and the nursing care lavished on the men when they were in hospital, but some wives, like Joan M, were concerned about their husbands' state of mind. When Joan M tried to discuss this with nursing staff at the Queen Elizabeth Military Hospital, Woolwich, she was assured her husband was 'stable'. But she knew that he had not yet experienced the delayed shock common to people who have survived a disaster in which others have died. She could not imagine what to expect of a man who had lived through the horrors of Bluff Cove and the pain of extensive burns. The Woolwich hospital doctors were 'not available' to discuss these worries with her, nor her husband's long-term medical care. She remembers his reaction as he watched a television news item on the fire-ravaged *Sir Galahad* being sunk as a war grave in the waters of the South Atlantic. For the first time since his return home he really gave vent to his feelings. Joan told me how he said he felt guilty at being alive when some of the young soldiers, whose families he personally knew, and whose brothers and sisters he had grown up with in Wales, had been killed. 'He felt he should have died too. I got angry then and said "What about me and the kids? Were we not worth living for?" He calmed down a bit but, months later, the guilt and the shock were still there.' They would be having a cup of tea and suddenly he would say 'I remember so and so.' One day he talked for three hours about what had happened, completely ignoring his wife who was in the room with him.

For some families, domestic tensions intensified when the injured did return home to convalesce. Soldiering is very much the work of young men and many of the injured had young wives who were already reeling from weeks of anxiety as well as coping with babies and toddlers. In hospital the wounded had received the undivided attention of nurses and doctors, and had the company of men in the same boat or worse off than themselves. There had been neither the time nor the privacy for too much introspection and their military discipline did not allow them openly to express their bottled-up fears and feelings, or lose face by breaking down in front of their colleagues. Once home, they had time to start thinking about what had happened to them and, like Joan's husband, and friends who had not come back. What they had experienced was something they could not share easily with a worried wife, and the insecurity about their futures did not help them handle the situation confidently. Many wives watched helplessly as their men oscillated between bouts of depression, anger, heavy drinking and occasional physical violence. Unmarried soldiers who had only bleak barrack rooms to return to preferred the company to be found in local pubs. When the right to 'light duties' meant, in the case of some of the injured Welsh Guards, the job of sorting out the personal effects of their dead friends, it is not surprising that a number of young squaddies really hit the bottle.

Wives like Tina Brookes still get angry about 'being forgotten and abandoned by the Army'. Her husband, Leslie, insists he is very lucky compared with some of his friends, who will never be able to live a near-normal life without a good deal of permanent help. After dental surgery to repair his mouth and gums, he went home to Sheffield to convalesce, but was diagnosed as having hepatitis and his weight loss and clinical depression were not helped by his constant anxieties for the future. No one he asked had been able to tell him what he and other wounded soldiers most wanted to know – how long would their medical treatment take, what future, if any, did they have with the Armed Forces, what was their financial position if they were medically discharged, and where would they, with three-and-a-half million unemployed, find work as disabled persons. Tina's baby was due just before Christmas; the couple were living temporarily with Tina's parents. This difficult situation was compounded by what Tina calls her husband's Jekyll and Hyde moods, which lasted for months after he came home, even after the birth of their daughter Rebecca. 'He was a really black and white personality and there were times when you did not know what to say to him. He would be sitting there quite normal and then fly off the handle for no reason.' One night his behaviour worried her so much that she phoned his father at three in the morning to come round and sort it out: 'I realise it wasn't anything to do with me personally, but I did not know how to stop it. There was the baby and sometimes I was very frightened.'

Leslie does not try to hide behaviour he says was common to many soldiers after the war, even those who were not injured, and refers to it in his forthright Yorkshire way as 'a right bad temper'. He did not sleep properly for months, which is not surprising after going with so little sleep in the Falklands, and he says his whole system was out of order from not eating regular meals and often fighting for hours on an empty stomach. But it was not just the lack of sleep and food: 'It was the experiences we went through that affected our bodies too.' At home, when he could sleep, he would often dream about what had happened. When he was awake and just sitting quietly, sometimes watching television, incidents would flash through his mind: 'It sent some people crazy. There was one from 3 Para who was medically discharged when he took to wearing an Argentine helmet he had brought back as a souvenir and jumping through plate glass windows.'

A year after the Falklands, Leslie Brookes had not really come to terms with the experience of doing what he had so expertly been trained to do – go to war and kill. It had seemed to him more like a holiday when they were on the North Sea ferry *Norland* en route with the rest of the task force to the South Atlantic. When they landed at San Carlos, the countryside was so like Dartmoor it felt like another military exercise. Seven days later came Goose Green and 'fighting hand to hand with bayonets, killing for real and your mates being killed next to you'. The thought that he, too, might die came, paradoxically, when he saw in the early morning light a young, dead Argentinian soldier lying in a trench as though he were asleep. 'He was clutching a crumpled letter, perhaps from his mother or wife, it might just as well have been one of us.' Leslie still talks of his Falklands War in terms of 'a bad dream'. The unreality was heightened by its brevity; there was just no time to adjust to rapidly changing circumstances, and within a fortnight of being shot on Wireless Ridge he came home and was supposed to get back to normal, 'just like that'.

In retrospect, barrack room routine was probably the quickest way for the military to restore some semblance of normality to the lives of young men still high on the unreality of their war experiences, but the injured could not take part in the comforting, cleansing and very physical rituals of normal Service life and their increasing sense of isolation and rejection is the cause of much bitterness still felt by those closest to them, who did not know how to help them or hit back at the system that was causing them so much distress.

Tina Brookes speaks for generations of soldiers' wives whose husbands came back injured from war when she says: 'He was one of Margaret Thatcher's "boys", a hero, but when it was over nobody wanted to know.'

CHAPTER FIVE:

The South Atlantic Fund

'The South Atlantic Fund did not have separate collecting boxes marked 10p for married men and 1p for single soldiers.' Gill Parsons, mother of an 18-year-old Falklands War casualty.

There was a predictable public response to the first casualties of the Falklands War. Within days of twenty crewmen being killed on HMS *Sheffield* on 4 May, the destroyer's adoptive city set up an appeal fund for the next of kin. Hereford, the home-base of the Special Air Service, did likewise for the nineteen local soldiers who died when their Sea King helicopter crashed into the waters of the South Atlantic after a freak collision with an albatross. Soon, money from all over Britain, and abroad, began to arrive at the Ministry of Defence offices in Whitehall, not only for the families of the men lost at sea but also the casualties on land after the D-Day embarkation of the task force at San Carlos on 21 May. The money was given in the same spirit that had brought a Union Jack-waving public to the docksides and coastal headlands of Britain's naval ports to give Woodward's motley armada such a resounding send-off. With money pouring in, the government felt it should be pooled into one fund, to prevent too much going to only a few families at the expense of dependents of future casualties. They also hoped their move would pre-empt further separate appeals being set up.

When John Nott announced the setting-up of the South Atlantic Fund on 25 May he defined it as a holding fund which would pass on the money to the existing Service charities for distribution. That very day the Argentines bombed the *Atlantic Conveyor* and the *Coventry* and thirty-two more men were killed; Nott's announcement did not stop the city of Coventry opening its own appeal for the bereaved families of the men lost on its adopted ship.

The South Atlantic Fund was the inspiration for such patriotic gestures as the promise by England's World Cup football team of a per centage of their pop record royalties. Dame Vera Lynn donated all of her royalties from a new record, *I Love This Land*, dedicated to the men of the task force. At a fund-raising auction for Falklands memorabilia, helicopter pilot Prince Andrew's flying gloves raised £500; the ceremonial top hat of Major General Mario Benjamin Menendez, the Islands' temporary Argentine governor, was knocked down for £5,000, while fifty acres of land given by the Falkland Island Company were bought for £2,500 by Cindy Buxton, one of the television wildlife film-makers marooned on the islands by the invasion.

It was only after the war that the stark realities of what had really happened in the South Atlantic began to appear on our television screens. Within hours of Margaret Thatcher announcing the ceasefire and crowds gathering outside Downing Street to sing *Rule Britannia*, delayed pictures were shown of the battlefield burials of the Goose Green dead, including 'H' Jones and his men. The black and white screen images were reminiscent of a newsreel from the Second World War. Even more harrowing was the television film of the fire-charred survivors staggering ashore at Bluff Cove from the still blazing *Sir Galahad*, and two grim-faced stretcher-bearers carrying a soldier whose blackened stump of a leg pointed skywards. The sobering impact of these pictures and the ground-swell of John Bullish pride that greeted the returning troops brought more money into the Fund. At the beginning of July it had reached £8 million; the final total, including investment capital, would top £16 million – a record for a publicly subscribed fund.

Controversy and bitterness have marked the recent handling of public funds in Britain, from Aberfan to the distribution of the Penlee Lifeboat Fund, just weeks before the Falklands War. The South Atlantic Fund was no exception. The war required an instant and generous response to the needs of families coping with death and injury. The money was there. But John Nott should really have known better than to hand that money over to any charity, never mind the Service charities. His Cornish constituency of St Ives covered the fishing village of Mousehole, which lost eight men aboard the lifeboat, *Solomon Brown*, in the Penlee disaster of December 1981. There was public outrage when it appeared that the £3 million given to the Penlee Fund might not be shared promptly among the bereaved, but hijacked by the Royal National Lifeboat Institution, to be dispersed strictly according to needs. When the Fund's Cornish trustees refused to hand the money to the charity, Margaret Thatcher had to ask her Attorney General to rule that equal sums be paid to the eight families. His new guidelines to charities were meant to prevent a repetition of the Penlee fiasco, and stressed that those organising an appeal should make sure that the purpose of the appeal is clear and that the donors know how their gifts will be used, so as to reduce the risk of confusion and distress. He also considered it undesirable to postpone decisions. He pointed out that such delays could lead both donors and beneficiaries to form the view that the 'ultimate result is not what was intended, as well as giving rise to legal problems'. From the start, those responsible for the South Atlantic Fund failed to comply with these guidelines. When Nott announced the setting-up of the Fund there was no hint about when the money would be spent, or how much would be given to the bereaved and injured. Just days before the 15 July, when donations had topped £8 million, a Trust Deed was drawn up giving the Fund the status of a charity. The Ministry of Defence admitted they had no idea how the money would be shared, but that it would be given to people 'in need', an ominous phrase with its undertones of means tests and State handouts.

The first five trustees selected by Nott were all men in their fifties and, but for one civil servant, they were top rank senior Service personnel – an Air Chief Marshal, an Admiral, a Second Sea Lord and a General. Prince Charles, who is the Colonel-in-Chief of numerous regiments, agreed to be the Fund's patron. A Royal Navy Captain, Anthony Lambourne, was seconded from a desk job as temporary secretary to the Fund, and installed with twenty staff from the three Services in Defence Ministry offices off Trafalgar Square.

With a captain at the helm and two of the trustees from the Royal Navy, the Fund was already dominated by a Service with no experience since the Second World War of dealing with the aftermath of a situation on the scale of the Falklands War. The Army at least were familiar with handling the death and injury of Servicemen in Northern Ireland. The Royal Navy was also the most formal and traditional of the three Services; its point blank refusal at first to allow journalists to sail with the task force was indicative of its secrecy, and a high-handed belief that it was not accountable to the press or the public. The age and rank of the trustees, compared with the average age of the task force men, speaks for itself. None of the Fund's decision-makers included those who would benefit from the public's generosity – no war-wounded, no widows or parents took part in the charity's deliberations.

When an established charity, the Royal British Legion, volunteered its administrative skills, it was rebuffed by the Whitehall-created team who were determined to do it their way. The decision to use the three parent Service charities – the King George's Fund for Sailors, the Army Benevolent Fund and the Royal Air Force Benevolent Fund – to distribute the money was their first mistake. It was a move that delayed the distribution of the money and revealed just how out of touch the Service charities were with the intention of those who had given money to the Fund, and the expectations of those who would receive it.

The Armed Forces are a male hierarchy based on a rigid rank structure. Their uniforms and traditions set them apart from civilian life. The men of the task force were better educated and more articulate than previous generations, who had compulsorily spent time in the Armed Forces. In the 1980s the Services were seen as a source of steady employment in the middle of a recession, and the men believed that whatever happened to them in the course of their duties they would be treated no better, or worse, by the powers-that-be than they would have been in civvy street. It was a shock to them to discover that when it came to dealing with the aftermath of a conventional war in 1982, the attitude of the Service charities and the Fund's trustees had not changed since the Second World War, when wounded veterans and widows were largely left to fend for themselves. It was an attitude embodied in the stoppage of allowances to wounded men who were unfit for duty because of their injuries, which defined the breakdown of a shell-shocked soldier as 'a grey area', and which seemed as though they could not imagine what additional expenses an amputee, or a badly burned Guardsman and his family, could have which were not already covered by the pay the Servicemen were still receiving.

The national headquarters of the three parent Service charities chosen by the Fund's trustees to distribute the money are run almost exclusively by retired senior Service personnel. They are a generation which reflects the attitudes of the most conformist section of the military hierarchy. They believe their work should be conducted, like their ex-Service careers, strictly by the rule book which, in this instance, meant sticking to the letter of charity laws which date back to 1601. The appeals secretaries for the Royal Air Force and Army Benevolent Funds were respectively an Air Commodore and a Brigadier, while the secretary of the King George's Fund for Sailors was Captain Edgar Brown, a doughty and forthright Royal Navy veteran, whose reply to my question about the possible means-testing of women widowed by the Falklands War was: 'I don't think the Falkland widows should find this humiliating; none of the other 13,000 or so widows from the Second World War and others we help find it humiliating.' It was this perspective, and a blinkered interpretation of Britain's outdated charity laws, under which beneficiaries first have to ask for help and then prove material needs, which led to the bottlenecks and bitterness in the distribution of monies from the Fund.

£10,000 interim grants for the 134 widows, and £1,000 each for their children, were paid by the end of August. All the widows and their children received the same tax-free payments, regardless of their circumstances, and the money was on top of the Service gratuities paid on their husbands' deaths, and their war widow pensions. This equal, interim payment, made without anyone having to ask for money or prove 'need', met with everyone's approval and it was assumed that future sums would be paid in the same way. The women appreciated the public's generosity; some were aware of the snide comparisons being made between their finances and those of Second

World War widows. To their critics, they replied that the public had given the money specifically for the problems created by the Falklands War, and they were not responsible for the plight of widows from other wars, for whose needs the State, and indeed the Services in which their men had given their lives, ought to have made adequate provision years before. However, the British War Widows Association, which did not begrudge the Falklands widows a penny, took the opportunity to highlight their still impoverished circumstances thirty-seven years after the last war.

An across-the-board payment of £2,500 each was also made by the Fund to the parents of the 121 single men killed in the Falklands War. This was on top of any gratuity already paid by the various Service insurance schemes, like ADAT, the Army Dependents Assurance Trust, which their sons might have taken out for their next-of-kin before leaving for the war. The Fund, as defined by its Trust Deed, is a holding fund, and did not pay money direct to the widows and parents. It reimbursed the relevant Service charities responsible for the welfare of the individual beneficiary. In addition to the three parent Service charities, there are a further 200 Service charities for specific regiments and groups, like the Welsh Guards Comfort Fund, the Gurkha Welfare Trust, Chinese Dependants, and Missions to Seamen. It was a bureaucratic and time-consuming way of dispersing agreed sums of money to so few, and involved separate bank accounts and book-keeping, which led to delays in some payments, when all could have quite simply been paid at the same time from the central Fund.

Once these interim sums were paid, the remainder of the Fund's money was placed in a bank deposit account while long-term investment plans were discussed.

At that stage, four months after the ceasefire, hardly a penny had been directly paid to the 777 war-wounded or their families, who were coping with the cost of travel and, in some cases, accommodation to visit their men in hospital, and the additional domestic expenses when their men returned home to convalesce. A few Service welfare officers, who had experience of similar situations after men had been injured on duty in Northern Ireland, took the initiative of giving small sums of money from regimental funds to those families who

99

were finding the unexpected expense of caring for their injured left them short. They also paid the travel costs for hospital visits and, in one instance, the bill for the adaptation of a car for a soldier who had had a leg amputated.

The attitude of the three parent Service charities was that while the war-wounded were receiving their pay they were all right for money. But should they, at a later date, be medically discharged with only an invalid pension, and the meagre sums paid by the government for their war injuries, then they might need a bit extra to help them adjust to civvy street, in which case they could apply for assistance and their needs would be carefully considered. What the three did not reveal was that they were *each* sitting on a quarter of a million pounds given them by the Fund in July to help the immediate needs of the injured and their families. Even more outrageous was that such a sum of money should have been given to, and accepted by, the RAF Benevolent Fund. The RAF had only one Falklands War casualty, whose widow and children had already been taken care of by the general Fund in the same way as the other widows and children.

It was humiliating to young men who had taken pride in their professionalism and been hailed as 'heroes' that their future needs should be dependent on the deliberations of a public charity. The Queen's Regulations made it impossible for them to protest publicly but, as a result of some interviews I had done about the impact of the war on people's lives, Servicemen's families contacted me at the *Sunday Mirror*. I approached a number of MPs, including Alf Morris, Labour's front bench spokesman on the disabled, to make some inquiries about the Fund and compensation to the war's wounded. Four months after the ceasefire, at a civic 'welcome home' reception for Servicemen in Plymouth, I introduced David Owen, the local MP for Devonport, to some war-wounded soldiers. He was horrified to learn that none of them had received a penny from the Fund. One man told him how, having lost a leg in the Falklands, he had to take out a loan to buy a car, as he could no longer use public transport or his bike to get to the barracks. The *Sunday Mirror*'s campaign for immediate interim payments to all the war's wounded was backed by MPs from all parties.

Stung by a critical *Sunday Mirror* editorial that described the

Fund's trustees as 'worthy brass hats', Captain Lambourne refused to answer my questions by telephone and summoned me to his office. In the presence of a minder from the Ministry of Defence Royal Navy press desk, whose Whitehall-issued tape recorder broke down, Lambourne revealed the real reason why money had not been paid immediately to the returning war-wounded. The interview, on 26 November 1982, which I have on my more reliable tape recorder, confirmed what I had suspected – that the Service charities had been dragging their heels at spending their windfalls from the Fund.

The day before, when Margaret Thatcher had told the House of Commons that the Fund had paid an estimated £1.5 million to the numerous Service charities, on behalf of the Falklands War wounded, she was clearly under the impression the money had actually been spent on them. When I asked Captain Lambourne how much had really reached anybody, as I knew of a number of seriously injured soldiers who had not got a penny, he said he would not know until the end of the month but added: 'We will top it up if necessary,' implying that he, too, believed that most of that money had already been spent. Later that day, following urgent questions by the Prime Minister's personal staff, Margaret Thatcher was told that only £345,000 had recently been given to the seventy-three most severely wounded, in payments ranging from £2,000 to £20,000. She angrily instructed that further interim sums be made 'at speed'.

The bottleneck had been caused by the Service charities who, as Captain Lambourne admitted, had turned round to the Fund's trustees, after taking their money, and said: 'We're looking after people from the Boer War, the First World War and the Second World War, or an accident that could happen in normal Service activities during peacetime, like helicopter crashes. People get killed, run over by tanks, you know, this sort of thing.' What it boiled down to was that the Falklands veterans could take their place in the queue , and when they could prove any material need they would be dealt with in the same way as a survivor from the Boer War.

Considering the age and background of the charities' senior staff their reasoning was not unexpected. To these retired Servicemen, who had personal contact with war-wounded

101

octogenarians who were ending their days in ex-Servicemen's rest homes, and were also familiar with the impoverished widows of earlier wars, the needs of the Falklands wounded, who were still receiving their pay, would not have appeared that pressing. Indeed, the whole of the Falklands conflict, a mere seventy four days from start to finish, must have seemed a decidedly rum and piffling affair compared with other wars, which had left thousands dead and injured.

The excuse that their charters restrained them from treating cases differently was no longer valid after the more flexible guidelines to charities given by the Attorney General, following the Penlee Lifeboat Fund fiasco. Also departure with tradition had already been set by the South Atlantic Fund itself, when it paid widows and bereaved parents interim sums without them having to ask for money or prove any need. This was heel-digging by the Service charities, in view of the generosity of the public who had given their money *specifically* for the Falklands. As Captain Lambourne ruefully commented: 'We were in a bit of a dilemma and had to set up a completely different approach.' Some money was eventually prised out of the service charities, but the renegades remained. At the end of 1983, when I asked the RAF Benevolent Fund's controller, Sir Alisdair Steedman, what they intended to do with their quarter of a million, given to them in the summer of 1982 for the Falklands casualties and their families – despite the fact that the RAF had only one war casualty – he said the money was still unspent and earning interest in an investment portfolio. What would eventually happen to it would depend on how, and when, the South Atlantic Fund was wound up. He declared: 'I am a heretic in that respect and feel the money should go into our general purpose fund.' That was never the intention of the donors.

The completely different approach Captain Lambourne had referred to was an attempt by the Fund individually to assess all the injured and bereaved. It meant someone from the welfare side of the Services, or their relevant charities, visiting them and discussing their personal circumstances, needs and future plans. A report was then sent to a Tri-Service Assessment Cell, made up of senior staff from the three parent Service charities and the Armed Forces, chaired by a major who was a lawyer. Medical reports and photographs of injuries were also submitted, and one of the guidelines for payments to the war-wounded was compensation paid by the Criminal Injuries Board to soldiers injured in Northern Ireland. The assessment panel recommended individual sums to the Fund's trustees, who authorised the payment through one of the Service charities. In practice, many families regarded the assessment as a means test and would not cooperate, some were never approached by anyone and had no idea how the sums of money they eventually received had been calculated, while the delays and discrepancies in payments caused even more upsets.

The discrepancies in payments to the widows, who had all received the same interim amounts, led to further complaints. Some widows like Maureen Emly, had refused to answer questions about her personal finances when a Royal Navy welfare officer called on behalf of the Fund at her Portsmouth home. She had no intention of being means-tested by a charity which had already given the widows the same payments. She told me: 'The whole idea was degrading and unnecessary. When I gave money to the Penlee lifeboat men's families I did not intend it to go to a charity to be doled out bit by bit when told someone was in need.' When Christina Heyes, whose twenty-one-year-old husband Stephen had died on HMS *Ardent*, was interviewed on behalf of the Fund by a voluntary worker for a Service charity, she became so upset by his attitude that a friend who was with her asked the man to leave. Christina remembered how the man made it clear he did not believe in the principle of the Fund, he was critical of the large amounts the widows were receiving, and said he thought her husband's family had as much claim to any future payments as she did, as the couple had only been married a year and were childless. He suggested she sell the house she and her husband moved into just days before he left for the Falklands, as it was now too big for her, and a flat would be cheaper to run. The mortgage on the house had been taken out with Stephen's wages and the money Christina had saved from doing two jobs at the same time, as a betting office cashier and an evening barmaid at a local pub. It was their first home and she had no intention of leaving it. Christina was asked to account in detail how she had spent the £10,000 interim sum – in fact, on renovating the house. His parting

103

shot was she might not get any more money and, therefore, ought not to expect any.

Equally traumatic was the cross-examination of one unmarried mother, whose lover had been killed in the war. She accepted that her claim had to be investigated before she could receive any more from the Fund, but at least expected to be treated with respect and sympathy. The young woman did not want to be identified because she had been warned by the Service welfare officer who visited her that speaking to the media could jeopardise her chances of payments from the Fund. She told me how a man from SSAFA, making inquiries on behalf of the Fund, had said she would be lucky to get anything as she was 'not a real widow'. The twenty-two-year old mother not only had a date set for her wedding to the father of her baby, but her future mother-in-law had made the bridesmaids' dresses. Although her vicar had written a letter on her behalf confirming the wedding plans, the SSAFA man insisted on visiting him personally, asked if she had ordered the wedding cake and rings, and poured over her dead lover's letters for any reference he might have made to their wedding and his child. He particularly wanted to see a photograph of them together as a family. The woman was able to show him a registered envelope and letter in which her lover had sent money to buy their child a pushchair. After further interviews by a Service welfare officer, the young woman did receive enough money to set up her own home, but said of her experiences: 'It was humiliating. Coming, as it did, on top of my shock and grief, it made me ill.'

The Fund was top heavy with Naval men and the Navy's hostility to press coverage of the Falklands War was just as apparent when it came to making the Fund and its trustees publicly accountable. Information on its deliberations and intentions was only given when MPs tabled questions and newspapers penned critical editorials. They did not voluntarily keep the public, the bereaved or the injured up to date with regular briefings. The Ministry of Defence information staff denied responsibility for inquiries on the Fund, especially when the flak flew; then they refused point blank to answer questions, insisting there was no working arrangement between the Ministry and the Fund, which was a charity run by trustees – all, of course, appointed by John Nott, who was party to the Fund's trust deed and was, therefore, just as accountable as the trustees.

In March 1983 a woman's magazine published an interview with Sara Jones, the widow of Lieutenant Colonel 'H' Jones VC, in which she criticised the Fund for keeping the public and beneficiaries in the dark about their intentions. She added: 'I also think that at least once a month a press statement should have been released detailing what was happening to the money. I don't think it has been handled very cleverly at all.' The weekend before the magazine went on sale the Fund promptly put out a statement that widows would eventually be paid between £30,000 and £50,000. It was certainly news to the majority, who had heard nothing since their interim payments the summer before. The much-publicised sums created expectations that for many were not fulfilled, and during the months that followed the differences in payments to women whose men had all been killed fighting the same war caused much anger and distress.

For various reasons, in some instances at their request, the women who received the following tax free payments are not named, but they were all at a loss to understand why their payments were so different. It is certainly difficult to justify the discrepancies in terms of the individual circumstances known to me. In addition to the interim payment of £10,000 for each widow and £1,000 for each child, the widow of a sergeant with two children received £20,000; the widow of a Welsh Guard who was pregnant with her first child when her husband died – £18,000; a Royal Navy officer's widow with one child – £26,000; the widow of a corporal with no children – £30,000; the widow of an able seaman with no children – £45,000; a Royal Navy officer's widow with three dependent children – £22,000; a Merchant Navy widow with two dependent children – £18,000; a sergeant major's widow with three children – £18,000. The final payments, including the interim grants, ranged from £30,000 to £70,000, the average being £38,000. The Fund refused to identify the rank and Service of the man whose widow received £70,000.

At one point it was incorrectly rumoured that widows of officers had received more because of their husbands' rank. This was not strictly true, as some childless widows of non-commissioned and lower ranks received far more than officers' widows. But the Army Officers Widows Fund did pay officers' widows £2,500 on top of any other money they received from the Fund, and these payments were reimbursed by the South Atlantic Fund. In effect, some officers' widows did receive more from the general Fund than others. But the total amounts they received were not necessarily higher than those of others.

When asked about the differences, the Fund's trustees said they were trying to make sure that families could lead the sort of lives they had expected if their men had not been killed, and they had based their assessments on the fact that some widows had suffered a greater financial loss as a result of their husbands' deaths than others. They also took into account State pensions and benefits, but not personal assets, private insurance or 'other similar personal provision'.

In 1982 the childless widow of a private soldier, who was under forty on her husband's death, received pensions from the DHSS and Ministry of Defence which jointly came to £2,700 per annum. She would also have received a gratuity, payable on death in service, of £7,500 to £10,500, depending on her husband's length of service. If these were her only sources of money then the onus was certainly on the Fund to make a generous payment – as they did to the childless able seaman's widow, who received a total of £55,000 – but, once again, as in the case of the war-wounded, it should not have been left to a public charity to make up for the inadequacy of statutory provision. The widow of a private with two children would have received a joint pension of £6,500. She would also have been paid the same gratuity as a childless widow. If these were her only sources of income, how can the Fund possibly justify her total payment of £30,000, which barely covered the cost of moving from Service quarters into a home of her own?

A stock reply from the Fund to any criticism about differences in payments was: 'As a Charitable Trust the Fund cannot make payments over and above those appropriate to need.' Surely the needs of a young widow with two children setting up her first home are self-evident, and required a sum over and above that awarded to a widow with no children, who already had a home of her own? And for the Fund to disregard personal assets makes complete nonsense of their insistence they can only make awards according to need. Just how do you define the needs of widows of senior ranking officers who received gratuities between £20,500 and £25,500 and a joint pension of £9,000 plus, with additional payments for any children? Their gratuities and pensions would be almost double that of a private's widow. If the latter received a total of £30,000 from the Fund, the logical conclusion would be that the needs of the former, with double her income, would justify a considerably lower sum. But the lowest sum paid to any widow was £30,000.

Many widows, having received the same interim grant, had assumed and would have welcomed that further payments were also made equally. They did not believe that a public charity should make up for the inadequacies of their other sources of income and, indeed, the two childless widows I knew, who had received more than some widowed mothers, were embarrassed and upset that they had received more. But what really distressed many families, including the parents of the single men who had been killed in the Falklands, who had been given nothing other than £2,500 each, was the very idea of a charity evaluating the deaths of their men on the basis of material circumstances and need. Marica McKay, whose husband Ian had posthumously been awarded one of the war's two Victoria Crosses, was so upset at the differences in payment to the families of men who had all died for the same cause that her mother-in-law, Freda, protested to Margaret Thatcher.

Freda had spent a lot of time with her daughter-in-law in Aldershot after Ian was killed. She had helped her settle into her own home after leaving married quarters with her daughter Melanie and son Donny. She often stayed at weekends when she came south from her Rotherham home to visit her youngest son, who was receiving hospital treatment in London for cystic fibrosis, which he and his other brother had suffered from all their lives. Ian's father, Ken, a steel metallurgist, had wanted the eldest of his three sons to stay on at school and become a games teacher, rather than join the Army when he was sixteen. But Ian had his father's Yorkshire stubbornness, and insisted on leaving home for the Parachute Regiment.

Ken and Freda McKay are only too aware of the poignant irony that their healthiest son, who had chosen such a physically demanding profession, should die in a totally unexpected war. Ian, together with other Servicemen who gave evidence to the Widgery Committee on the events they were caught up in on Bloody Sunday in Londonderry in 1970, had been excused further duties in Northern Ireland for security reasons. Bar accidents during the Paras rigorous training course he put the rookies through as an instructor at Aldershot, his family no longer regarded his career as any more dangerous than the work some of their colleagues did in the local Sheffield steelworks. Ian's two brothers, Graham and Neil, had been devastated by the death of Ian who, when they were children, had protected them, because of their illness, from the more boisterous activities of their friends. Freda McKay, while proud of her son's Victoria Cross, told me that if anyone deserved awards for courage they are her younger sons, who have coped all their lives with ill-health. She saw Ian's reaction to the situation for which he won the VC as perfectly natural to him, given his sense of responsibility to the young soldiers in his platoon, some of whom he had trained personally. It was the same sort of protectiveness he had felt towards his kid brothers. She said: 'There was never anything of the hero in Ian. If he saw something that had to be done he would do it. Ian had a lot of young lads with him and he would feel responsible for their safety.'

Freda is a quietly-spoken, thoughtful woman, at forty-nine years old only sixteen years older than her daughter-in-law, and they became close the year following Ian's death. It was through Marica she met some of the other young Para widows. She was angry at the discrepancies in payments to young mothers setting up their own homes away from married quarters, who had received less than the Fund's much publicised average of £38,000, never mind £50,000 or £70,000.

The widows were worried that their criticism of the Fund might be seen by the public as a squabble among themselves about differences in payment. They appreciated the public's generosity and did not want to appear ungrateful, but they would have preferred to have all received the same amount and had done with it. As Marica told me, no one had dared to come to means-test her, or any of the other women she knew, so on what basis had the Fund assessed their needs and future plans? Freda was conscious that the family name might have some impact on public opinion and, as she did not personally benefit from the Fund, she decided to speak for them and the injured men, who were so worried about the future. At a later date, she spoke up for the parents of the single men. She made public her letter to Margaret Thatcher, in which she asked that whatever money was left in the Fund should be divided equally as soon as possible between the widows and the injured.

Margaret Thatcher's reply was predictable. She quoted the charity laws which, she said, required the Fund to make payments on the basis of need, and continued: 'Like you, I honour the sacrifice made by every man who fell on behalf of his country in the Falklands campaign. I do not think it detracts from that honour that some widows have suffered a greater financial loss as a result of their husbands' deaths than others.' Freda was disappointed; she described the reply as impersonal, but: 'Very much what I expected. She really had not grasped what I was getting at, which was that each man's death was of equal value in the eyes of the people who had given their money to the South Atlantic Fund and that the money should have been shared equally, like the Penlee Lifeboat Fund. If her government had been prepared to make an exception under the charity laws for the Penlee families, they could do so again.'

Freda's reasoning was the nub of an appeal made to the Fund by the Association of Parents of Unmarried Sons, which represented 60 families of the 121 single men killed in the Falklands. The Association was formed during the return journey home from the islands by those who went on the government-arranged visit in April 1983.

If anything could really upset the secretary of the Fund and its trustees it was the criticisms levelled at them by the parents. Rosemary Anslow, whose son Adrian had died on the *Atlantic Conveyor*, told me of a meeting she and her husband had with Captain Anthony Lambourne at their hotel the night before they left for the Falklands. Rosemary told him how she believed the public had given money to the Fund to compensate all the families equally for their loss, and the £2,500 they had received for the death of their only son was an insult. She remembered that Captain Lambourne had replied that if that was the way she felt why did she not refund the money; it had only been given because the trustees had decided to make a concession, but by law the parents should not have got a penny. Rosemary had turned away the two men from the Royal Navy who had called at her Wolverhampton home on behalf of the Fund to assess her needs. She told them: 'There is only one thing I need and that is my son; you cannot assess that in terms of money. Adrian was only twenty when he died; he did not have the privilege of being married and having children, but all the men who were killed were valued the same by the public, whether married or single.'

It was a powerful and emotive plea and one I heard time and again from many parents, including Gill Parsons, whose eighteen-year-old Welsh Guardsman son had been killed on the *Sir Galahad*. She told me angrily: 'The Fund did not have separate collection boxes marked 10p for married men and 1p for single soldiers. Why is one life worth more than another? I was told we were not being compensated for our grief, and that anyway a wife would miss her husband more than a mother would miss her son.' An argument to which Theresa Burt would reply: 'A widow can replace her husband if she wishes, but a mother may never replace her child.' Theresa would still like someone to explain to her why a fellow soldier of her seventeen-year-old son Jason received £7,500 from the Fund for a damaged hand, when she and her husband had received only £2,500 for the death of their son. When Pat Stockwell read a letter from the Mayor of Coventry in the Navy News that £54,670, out of a total of £77,000 raised by the city's appeal, had been spent on some of the families of the Servicemen who died on their adopted ship, she wondered why no one had contacted them. Their only son Geoffrey had been one of the twenty casualties and yet she and her husband Leslie, the chairman of the Parents Association, heard of the Coventry appeal quite by chance. She told me: 'Nothing could ever compensate us for the loss of our son, but it is difficult to imagine the citizens of Coventry intended the sacrifice of single men on their adopted ship should have been totally ignored.'

None of the Association's parents have ever questioned the priority given by the Fund to the widows and the wounded, but they feel they should have received something more from whatever remained in the Fund. This is clearly not the intention of the trustees, who are determined to share the £2 million plus residue among the Service charities, including those who have not yet spent the earlier sums of money given to them. It is a move that Janet Stuart, the secretary of the Parents Association, is equally determined to resist. Her eldest son Matthew died on his eighteenth birthday on HMS *Argonaut* during the landings at San Carlos Bay. The young weapons handler was in the missile magazine at the bow of the ship when it was hit by two bombs which failed to explode. One bomb hit the ship below the waterline and passed through a fuel tank into the Sea Cat Missile magazine, triggering local explosions, although it did not detonate itself. Matthew and another weapons handler in the area were killed instantly.

Before Matthew's death his mother had helped her husband Ray run their own business, selling fancy goods to shops and stores. For weeks after Matthew died his father could not bring himself to do anything, or meet anybody. They lost their business and a lot of their savings. It took Ray Stuart over a year to pull himself out of the depression and shock to find a job as an area salesman. Janet Stuart says that too few people have considered the effects of the Falklands War on families like hers, that the public hear only of the widows and their children, but many fathers, as well as mothers of married sons, have been devastated by the unexpected and violent nature of their children's deaths. She seeks recognition from the Fund that her son's life really was worth as much as that of other Servicemen who died in a war which, after her visit to the Falklands she felt was a waste of anyone's life, British or Argentine. She intends to take the parents' case for further money from the Fund to the Strasbourg-based Commission on Human Rights.

It is a move Captain Edgar Brown would find incomprehensible. As secretary of one of the Fund's parent Service charities, he was a member of their assessment panel, and held the purse strings to both the *Coventry* and *Sheffield* appeal funds, which respectively raised £77,000 and £147,000 and were handed over to the King George's Fund for Sailors. Final payments to families who lost men on the two sister ships were jointly financed by all three funds. The redoubtable captain said he would have had nothing to do with any of the Funds if the money had been shared equally among the bereaved and

111

injured. He told me: 'Equal shares and compensation are not words we use in charity. I have a clear conscience that we have done the right thing.' He was at pains to point out that more seamen lose their lives at sea every year than the total number of lives lost in the Falklands War, and the families of those men would never benefit in the same way as those who received money from the South Atlantic Fund. He continued: 'I have 1,000 merchant navy widows on my books whom we can only afford to pay £2.50 a week; compared with the Falkland widows they are very badly off.'

Given his perspective, Captain Brown has certainly done the honourable thing by sticking to the charity rule book, but it is unfair to compare the poverty of 1,000 merchant navy widows with the resources of the Falklands widows. The people who gave their money to the South Atlantic Fund did so for families devastated by the Falklands War. There really should be no need for such funds in the first place, or the 200 and more Service charities who doggedly dispense their largesse according to centuries-old rules that smack of poor laws. The State should provide adequate pension and insurance schemes to cover the needs of Armed Forces dependants and war-wounded men. It is a disgrace that 1,000 merchant navy widows should be beholden to Captain Brown's charity for £2.50 a week – but what has his generation done about making the government responsible for taking care of their needs?

Colonel John Ansell, who succeeded Captain Lambourne as the secretary for the South Atlantic Fund, referred to the parents' request for equal payments as 'naive'. Captain Brown and his colleagues have declared their intention of pooling any more money they receive from the South Atlantic Fund into their general coffers, although they cannot spend the Fund's money on anything other than Falkland War-related cases until 1987 when, according to the Fund's trust deeds, it is scheduled to be wound up. What still remains of their original £250,000 windfalls, given for the immediate needs of the war-wounded, is now earmarked for their long-term needs, should anyone ever dare to make a claim. What will eventually happen to the RAF's untouched £250,000, gathering capital in its investment portfolio, is anybody's guess.

The unshakeable belief of the Service charities that they have behaved correctly, and should never have been questioned about their conduct in the first place, was evident in the reply from Brigadier Lanyon, the appeals secretary of the Army Benevolent Fund. When I asked him how much of his £250,000 emergency grant remained, almost eighteen months after the ceasefire, he replied: 'We have spent substantially more than the £100,000 accounted for earlier this year. But we are not prepared to say how much, or what we give people, and who we give it to. To talk of individual cases is confusing, the public just do not understand.'

The trust deeds permit the Fund to be wound up and its residue dispersed by 1987. The trustees' current intention is to hand over that money to the Service charities, who will place it in their general pools, and any future Falklands War claimant will have to prove need in the same way as a Boer War veteran or a Second World War widow. That was never the intention of those who gave money to the Fund. Colonel Ansell could not satisfactorily explain to me why the Fund, whose trustees have insisted that, under the charity laws, they could only make payments to individuals after 'means testing' their material needs, had paid £11,400 towards the conversion of a building for use as an airmen's club on Ascension Island, and for some of the club's sports and video equipment, when £250,000 of the Fund's money was still lying unused in an RAF investment portfolio. And under what definition of 'need' did the Army Benevolent Fund pay £2,000, reimbursed by the Fund, for the airfares of three Falklands war-wounded going on a 42-day remedial visit to Australia? An Antipodean holiday for wounded soldiers was certainly a refreshing reversal of Captain Lambourne's concern that too much money, given too soon to the injured, might result in 'dissipation'. He told me that medical advice to the Fund included the dire warning that rehabilitation could be disrupted by giving the wounded large sums of money, and quoted an example supplied to him by BLESMA (with whom they were now on speaking terms, after initial refusals to take on board their expertise) of a young Serviceman – not a Falklands veteran – who had lost a leg, had family problems, took to drinking and eventually committed suicide.

The Fund's misplaced desire to protect war-wounded men

113

from themselves might just have been plausible if they had made any effort at all to talk to the Servicemen's families about the problems they had been left to cope with alone.

CHAPTER SIX:

Compensation For Heroes

'People can see when a man has lost an arm or a leg, but nobody can see what a war does to a man's mind.' Gillian White, wife of a shell-shocked Falkland veteran.

Tina Brookes' anger at the military and civil authorities for ignoring the problems she and her injured husband were having to face alone was shared by many families once the Falklands casualties returned to their own homes and married quarters. The expense of living with their injuries caused even more domestic problems. Working wives took unpaid leave or gave up jobs to stay at home and nurse their men or spend the best part of the day with them in hospital. At home there were the additional costs of providing extra meals, heating and special clothing – soldiers whose burns were still being treated daily with medicated creams could only wear cotton fabrics next to their painfully sensitive skin. One wife borrowed £300 from relatives to buy five complete sets of cotton clothes for her Welsh Guard husband, clothes that were changed and laundered twice a day as the skin creams soaked through. Men with amputations had to pay for taxis to get anywhere, as they could no longer drive their cars or manage public transport while they were still getting used to artificial limbs.

An Army camp is very like a village, an enclosed community where neighbours know each other's business and problems. Regimental officers must have been aware of the hardships some families faced, but too few did anything. Numerous regiment and Service charities exist to help families in these circumstances and the South Atlantic Fund gave £250,000 each to the three principal Service charities specifically to help the injured. Four months after their return from the Falklands hardly a penny of that money had been spent on them, because charity rules insist that payments can only be made to those who apply for help and can prove they need assistance. In the all-knowing parish pump atmosphere of barrack room life, no one was going to belittle themselves by asking for charity or telling the regiment's pay master they had money problems. The women felt helpless; it was the 'system' to blame and nobody could do anything about it. But their frustration exploded in public anger when the 'system' penalised their men for their war injuries by deducting much-needed allowances from their wages because they were medically unfit for duty. These savage cuts were something that really hit the family purse, already stretched by additional expenses for caring for the injured. After weeks of anxiety, the women really had something on which to focus their bitterness and they decided to fight back.

The first hint of allowances being stopped to the injured came from the Parachute Regiment at Aldershot. News leaked out of £45 a month being deducted from the wages of wounded and limbless soldiers who could no longer do parachute duties. The Ministry of Defence hit the roof at the publicity, furiously reminding commanding officers that no one must talk to the media without their permission. The Ministry was still smarting from some very justified criticism in Fleet Street on the way they had handled the news coverage of the war. Paranoid that the press was about to embarrass them further with sob stories about the war's wounded, they made it clear to newspapers inquiring about the stoppages that Servicemen could only give interviews in the presence of a 'minder' from the Ministry or the regiment. They signalled all COs to remind their officers, and in turn all ranks, that talking to the press without permission was a breach of the Queen's Regulations and they would be disciplined. These regulations govern the conduct of the Armed Forces and forbid Servicemen to speak to the media without the permission of their commanding officer. But even with clearance from their superiors they may only discuss factual matters and cannot engage in political debate or criticism of the Services. The ruling effectively gags all Servicemen from giving their personal opinions and is totally unacceptable in a society where the military, at every level, should be publicly accountable.

Servicemen may still be used to doing what they are told, but today's generation of Service wives are not. When the £1.42p a day London living allowance was retrospectively docked from the pay packets of forty-four wounded Guardsmen at Chelsea Barracks, in some instances halving a month's wages, their wives refused to stay silent. The women spoke of their anger in a number of letters and telephone calls to me at the *Sunday Mirror*, where I had started a campaign for immediate interim payments to the injured from the £16 million South Atlantic Fund. Their letters were a poignant mix of patriotism, pride and protectiveness. They were very concerned that their protests should not rebound on their men and for that reason asked the newspaper not to publish their names. One wife who had given up her job to be at home while her husband recovered from a leg amputation, wrote: 'Since my husband was injured on 12 June we have had no one approach us to even inquire as to our financial needs. Thank God we have been able to manage. These men wounded in action are proud men who would never dream of asking for charity. At the end of October, life was made a little bit harder due to the fact that Army regulations state that during a period of hospital care my husband is not entitled to our London living allowance and has in fact had deducted from his wages the sum of £1.42p a day backdated to his arrival back in the UK. I ask you what price bravery and disability? I remain tremendously proud of my husband's part in the Falklands' War and want no part in asking for charity. I remain anonymous as my husband and I are repeatedly told not to speak to the Press, but I can no longer sit back and accept the treatment dished out to my husband and many like him. I think the phrase should be – Lest We Forget.'

Another letter writer, summarised the feelings of many families: 'For a man who fought for his Queen and country he is actually paying for his own injury. These men were only too proud to fight for their country and I think it's time the people of Great Britain should be told exactly what is happening to the injured who fought for them so bravely. I cannot give my name and address because the powers that be have asked us not to get in touch with the Press. But I feel so strongly about this I thought it my duty to write and express my feelings. My husband is still under the hospital and I dread to think how much more his injury is going to cost us.'

Other women at the barracks told me of a young wife with three children whose wounded husband had been in hospital since his return from the Falklands. After the stoppage of their living allowance the young mother was so short of money she could not pay her food bills. Her family sent her the train fare to go home to Scotland and live temporarily with her mother. She never returned to London. At a time when her injured husband was most in need of his wife and children, money problems had forced the young woman to put the children first. With the maximum stoppage of £234.50p in backdated allowances deducted from the injured soldiers' October pay – which averaged £360 for privates, up to £450 a month for sergeants – there was little money to spare to help others, even if they had asked neighbours for help. Some families took out loans to pay household bills or got advances on their next pay cheques. The stoppages caused such a stir in the barracks that problems cannot have gone unnoticed by the regiment's welfare officers. It is disturbing that no one appears to have taken the trouble to investigate possible hardship at a time when injured men were at their most vulnerable – still receiving medical treatment, worried about their future as soldiers, or how, as disabled men in civvy street, they could provide for their families if they were medically discharged from the regiment.

Even more disturbing is a situation that forces people to write unsigned letters to newspapers in a last-ditch attempt to right a wrong. Just what sort of system is it in which protest and criticism must be anonymous because of fear of reprimand? A swingeing rule which penalises men for being wounded is so patently unjust that any fair society would insist the rule be changed. But it seems that in the cloistered world of the Armed Services there are practices that do not permit public scrutiny. Paradoxically, it was to defend the principles of a fair and democratic society, including the freedom of speech, that Britain went to war against a military dictatorship. But what price democracy at home when a limbless war veteran is penalised financially for his injury and threatened with disciplinary action if he uses his right of free speech to complain?

The official comment from the Defence Ministry was coldly non-committal: 'The London weighting allowance of £1.42p a day payable to all ranks is to compensate soldiers for the problems and difficulties of working in the London area. Consequently, if the soldier is not able to perform his duties because he is in hospital or on a sick list he is not paid.' When the report appeared in the *Sunday Mirror* on 21 November, the public response and fury of some Members of Parliament soon changed the Ministry's tone. Within twenty-four hours they had fallen back to their stock whipping boy, a 'callous computer' which was to blame for this 'heartless action'. What that failed to explain was why the living allowances had been stopped four months after the injured returned from the Falklands – it was almost as though someone in Whitehall had belatedly spotted the allowances were still paid to the injured, checked the rule book and docked them retrospectively from the next pay slips. An indication that the callous computer would restore the allowances came a week later, on 29 November, in a written reply to MP Alfred Morris, Labour's spokesman on the disabled. The letter from Jerry Wiggin, Under-Secretary of State for the Armed Forces, not only promised the allowances would be paid back in full but the rules changed 'so that when a London-based Serviceman is in hospital, on sick leave, or undergoing medical treatment he will continue to receive his London pay supplement'. When the Defence Ministry released these details on 30 November, the BBC made it the lead item on their radio news bulletins. The soldiers' wives had not only scored a victory, but found a very public voice.

It was just the incentive needed for focusing public attention on what was happening to the Falklands injured. Not only did more wives and mothers feel they could legitimately ignore the 'don't talk' orders issued to their soldier husbands and sons, but it gave the men themselves confidence to complain to their regiments about their treatment and demand some action, particularly about plans for their future role in the Services.

It had not taken long for the Falklands war-wounded to realise that if the South Atlantic Fund did not recognise their financial needs, there would be no other source of compensation for their injuries than the paltry sums payable by the government when they were medically discharged. If they had been injured on duty in the streets of Northern Ireland, or even off-duty at home in Britain by a terrorist bomb, they would have been able to claim compensation under the Criminal Injuries Compensation Scheme. Indeed, in some cases, they would have been better off if they had received their injuries as civilians in a back street mugging in their own home town, than on a bloody battlefield.

In Northern Ireland British troops help the Security Services combat terrorism and quell civil disturbances. Servicemen can be compensated for their injuries in the same way as civilians caught up in terrorist incidents under the Criminal Injuries Compensation (Northern Ireland) Scheme. The Northern Ireland office refuses to give figures for the number of British soldiers who have received compensation for their injuries while serving in the Province, nor will they be drawn on individual sums paid to any Serviceman. A total of £72 million has been paid to 44,000 people in Northern Ireland for personal injuries resulting from civil disturbances in the past twelve years. It is on record that a British soldier, shot in Londonderry in 1973, was two years later awarded £15,000 compensation under the criminal injuries scheme for the loss of a leg above the knee. A senior Army officer, who did not wish to be named, told me that payments up to £45,000 for permanent disabilities were made to victims of the Warrenpoint ambush on 26 August 1979, in which eighteen soldiers were killed just hours after an IRA bomb, planted in a motorboat in Donegal Bay, killed Earl Mountbatten and three others. A Guardsman, who lost three limbs in the 1975 Caterham pub bomb, was eventually awarded £95,000 by the Criminal Injuries Compensation Board, London.

In 1982 the government's compensation to a Falklands veteran, with less than five years' service, medically discharged with a permanent disability, such as the loss of a leg below the knee, would have been £1,487. The average compensation paid by the British government under the criminal injuries scheme to civilian victims of a terrorist knee-capping in Northern Ireland was £1,500. Consultant surgeon Willoughby Wilson OBE, of Belfast's Royal Victoria

Hospital, insists that knee-capping is a misnomer: 'The knee-cap is rarely injured, nor is the joint. And there is rarely serious arterial or nerve damage to give a chap a permanently disabled limb.' (The wound, which is usually to the soft thigh tissue, is intended to hurt and frighten the victim and eventually heals.)

In 1982 the government's payment to a Falklands veteran with less than five years' service, medically discharged because of a one hundred per cent disability, such as total blindness or the loss of both hands, would have been £2,974. The year before, the Criminal Injuries Compensation Board in Belfast awarded a forty-seven-year-old man £100,000 for the loss of a leg and partial deafness, injuries resulting from a sectarian bombing. Higher payments than the base rate for private soldiers are given according to rank and service: but the average age of the task force soldier was nineteen, and many of the Falklands veterans had been in the Services for less than three years.

When I tried to discuss the difference in payments to Servicemen with the same injuries, but sustained in different military engagements – the Falklands War and Northern Ireland – I was given a classic Ministry of Defence reply. A spokesman said: 'You cannot compare the sums on offer for injuries received in the Falklands with compensation paid to soldiers in Northern Ireland. Compensation implies money given because of ill-luck or the culpability of another party. Payments for injuries in the Falklands are entitlements awarded to Servicemen because they are called upon to put their lives at risk in the course of duty.' There are few Servicemen who would make such a fine distinction between an Argentine bullet and one fired from the gun of the IRA terrorist.

No one was aware of these differentials until four months after the ceasefire, when the Falklands wounded began to ask questions about what would happen to them if they were medically discharged. Many of the wounded were young married men, living in Service quarters and only too aware that their injuries would make it even harder for them to find work in the middle of a recession. Their wives were desperately worried about the future; no one had reassured them that their men would not be compulsorily discharged and

121

given notice to quit their Service homes. It did not help when they realised that government compensation for their injuries would hardly help them start a new life in civvy street. The men's superior officers were equally in the dark about the intentions of the South Atlantic Fund and, also, could not air the issues publicly because of the Queen's Regulations.

I had written a number of articles on the impact of the war on task force families and, given the composition of the *Sunday Mirror* readership, it was only a matter of time before the wives and mothers of Falklands casualties began to telephone and write to me for help and advice. With so much money sitting around in the South Atlantic Fund, there was an obvious short-term solution to the inadequacy of government provision for the war-wounded. When I discussed the situation with Alf Morris, Labour's front bench spokesman on the disabled, he was appalled that the futures of young men, so recently hailed as heroes, were now dependent on the largesse of a public charity. He agreed to ask a number of questions in the House of Commons, and to press for immediate interim payments to the wounded from the fund. There was tremendous cross-bench support for the *Sunday Mirror*'s campaign; both David Owen and Winston Churchill were highly critical of the Fund's inertia and the foot-dragging that had gone on within the Service charities.

Six months after her son Mark had returned home with his left arm torn apart by shrapnel, his widowed mother, Dorothy Blain, asked me if he qualified for anything from the Fund, as he had not yet received a penny from anyone. I knew a Guardsman, with a similar injury to Mark's, who had just received an interim payment of £2,000 from the Fund. It was not until the end of January 1983, six weeks after I had spoken to the Fund about Mark, that he got a cheque for £500. Mark, a private with the 3rd Battalion Parachute Regiment, had given up a job with the Post Office in Liverpool to join the Paras. It was a schoolboy ambition which he had postponed after his bus driver father died of a heart attack, until he was sure his widowed mother could cope on her own with his younger brother and sister. His battalion were among the first soldiers to disembark at Port San Carlos on 21 May; they had advanced on foot across the islands and Mark had survived the forty-eight hour siege of Mount Longdon, in which

3 Paras' casualties were twenty-three men killed and forty-seven injured. The day before the war ended on 14 June, and within sight of Port Stanley, Mark was thrown twelve feet into the air and twenty feet sideways by a mortar shell blast. His friends were amazed he landed in one piece. In spite of the surgical skills of military doctors, Mark's left arm is useless; he can move only a couple of fingers and, almost two years after the war, still occasionally experiences intense pain.

When I visited him at his mother's home in Liverpool, soon after his medical discharge in March 1983, the wall above the sitting room gas fire was a testimony to his brief career as a soldier. Between two battalion plaques was a framed citation presented for outstanding service with the 7 platoon C Company, which read: 'During the Falkland campaign you performed admirably under fire, and even when wounded were an inspiration to all. Your services have been marked by a selfless attitude and willingness to expend every effort to achieve superior results.' Dorothy Blain had proudly hung her son's South Atlantic campaign medal above the citation, and his red Para beret underneath. Among family photographs on a nearby record player was one of Mark with the late Sergeant Ian McKay VC, his platoon sergeant during his six-month training in Aldershot.

Mark, who was registered at the local job centre, angrily told me: 'I am on the unemployed disabled register, but everyone seems to have their quota of disabled people. I am twenty-three, and it is not the same as being an unemployed school-leaver. I have always worked and, for two years with the Paras, had a totally satisfying career. Everyone said, given my circumstances as a Falklands War veteran, someone would offer me work. But why should anyone bother to give a job to a bloke with a gammy arm, when there are three and a half million able-bodied unemployed to choose from?' Mark was not bitter about what had happened to him as a soldier; he accepted that as part of his job and was proud to have fought for his country. But he was bitter that no one wanted to know what was now happening to him, or had given him any help and advice about his future. No one had even bothered to tell him what statutory benefits and pensions he was entitled to as a disabled war veteran. He had been left completely in the dark.

It was not until June 1983, a year after the war ended, that Lieutenant Paul Allen circulated an information pack to the War's disabled. The young Royal Marine, who has since left the Services, lost a foot in the Falklands. He had been seconded to the South Atlantic Fund after criticism of the trustees' ignorance of the immediate needs of the war-wounded. His introductory letter, written on Ministry of Defence headed notepaper, read: 'Gentlemen, as an amputee myself, I have *recently* become aware of the general lack of knowledge among the disabled from Operation Corporate as to their rights, and the various benefits/allowances and pensions for which they qualify. Consequently I enclose a pack which I hope goes some way to resolving this problem.' The pack contained information on the rights of the disabled, war pensions and allowances, and advised amputees to write to the British Limbless Ex-Servicemen's Association and subscribe to their quarterly magazine, BLESMAG. This was a complete policy reversal of the Fund's and the Defence Ministry's refusal the year before to cooperate with the voluntary organisation, when it offered its expertise to the Falklands War injured.

Mark knew the sort of compensation he could have received for his injury if he had been wounded in Northern Ireland. He also knew of the considerably higher sums than the Fund's £500 cheque sent him at the end of January 1983, which had been paid to fellow Paras for injuries far less serious than his. He had pinned all his hopes on enough capital from the Fund to buy his own home with a small business, such as a newsagents. His mother and girlfriend were very worried about his bouts of anger and depression, aware that it was not only the nagging pain that triggered off his introspection, but a sense of rejection and isolation, and acute anxiety about his future. It was not until eighteen months after the war ended that Mark Blain, still unemployed through no fault of his own, got a final settlement from the Fund – a cheque for £44,000.

It was thirteen months after the ceasefire that Para Leslie Brookes received £3,000 for a permanent facial scar, the result of a mouth injury that needed painful and complicated surgery. By then he had left the Services, was unable to find a job and, only with the help of both their families, had managed to put together a home for himself, his wife Tina and their baby Rebecca. The money would have been welcome much earlier. When ex-Marine Kevin Woodford, who had deposited an interim payment with a local building society of £5,000 from the Fund, for the loss of his leg, approached them about a mortgage for a house which he and his wife Angie hoped to buy, they turned him down because he could get no written confirmation from anyone on how much more he might receive from the Fund, and when it would be paid. It was more than a year after the war ended that he received a final payment of £70,000.

The sums of money paid to Mark, Leslie and Kevin were comparable to those made to Servicemen for similar injuries by the Criminal Injuries Board in Northern Ireland. But it was a public charity which paid £67,000 to a paratrooper who lost his leg below the knee in the Falklands; from the government he would have received £1,487 when medically discharged. The Falklands War veterans only received payments comparable to those made to Servicemen in Northern Ireland as a result of their own muted protest, made public for them by their women, rather than any initiative taken by the government. Once the interim payments had been made, the delays in final settlements – in some cases assessments are still being made – were inexplicable, when guidelines for payments on similar injuries already existed in Northern Ireland. To plead, as the Fund occasionally did, that long-term assessments of needs had to be made, is inexcusable. In the 1980s the long-term needs of war-wounded men should not be left to the deliberations of a charity. Surely the government that sent them to war is ultimately responsible for those future needs? The final casualty list was remarkably low, given the devastating effect of modern warfare. If it had been far worse, then the government would have had to find money to compensate the injured at the same rate as their brother soldiers wounded in Northern Ireland, or there would have been a public outcry.

The government was spared that embarrassment and the Falklands Factor, so invaluable to their re-election, remained intact. But it is inexcusable that a generation after the Second World War the government still does not provide adequate compensation for its war injured – and this time it was let off the hook by a public charity.

In 1984 there are still Falklands veterans receiving medical treatment who do not know what their final payment from the Fund will be, and whose future in the Services is unpredictable because of the delayed effects of their injuries. Lance Corporal Andrew Wallis* joined the Royal Engineers hoping to learn a trade. He had no time to take up his apprenticeship as a carpenter in April 1982 before leaving for the Falklands. He returned home with twenty-six per cent burns to his body and face, his badly charred hands still wrapped in plastic bags. Two years later he had to abandon all plans to be a carpenter because his scarred skin is sensitive to the dust, polish and the cleaning fluids used in his chosen trade. He was still in the Royal Engineers, and receiving medical treatment for his burns at the Queen Elizabeth Military Hospital, Woolwich. He had been given a total of £4,000 by the South Atlantic Fund. On both occasions the cheques were paid soon after I had spoken about delays to the Fund's secretary. A married soldier with two children, at the same barracks as Andrew, had received £65,000 from the Fund for only slightly more serious burns to his hands. Last October Andrew married his girlfriend Ann, a state registered nurse, and they expect their first child this summer. Ann gave up her job because of a difficult pregnancy, and to move to married quarters near the Royal Engineers' Maidstone barracks. They have no idea what the future holds for them; Andrew has not been told how much longer his medical treatment will last, or what sort of job he will be given if he stays in the Army.

Ann told me that when Andrew and his injured colleagues returned from the Falklands they were asked if they wanted a medical discharge: 'It was obvious the Services did not know what to do with them. But they were so worried about their job prospects in civvy street they decided to stay on until they had finished their hospital treatment.' She described how, a month before the first anniversary of the *Sir Galahad* bombing, she had lost her ability to concentrate on her work. Since Andrew's return from the Falklands War Ann had devoted herself almost exclusively to getting him better; the war, and how he had received his injuries, was 'just one black hole, we never talked about it'. Andrew responded to the newspaper and television coverage of the war's first anniversary with

*Although Andrew was still in the Services, the family wanted to be identified, regardless of the Queen's Regulations.

what Ann and his mother call 'the wobblers'. His condition was not helped by the job he had been given in the camp's bedding and clothing store, where he spent hours on his own, with little to do, and no one to talk to. His wife and mother were so concerned about him they telephoned Woolwich hospital and suggested he perhaps ought to see a psychiatrist. They also asked that Andrew not be told about their call. Andrew was not only told his family had telephoned the hospital, but he denied there was anything wrong with him. Soon after, he was transferred to a bar steward's job in the officers' mess.

Six months later, Andrew Wallis was again a patient at Woolwich waiting for further assessment. He had heard nothing more from the South Atlantic Fund, and his wife did not know what would eventually happen to them, as no one they had asked was prepared to talk to them about their future. She believed that the constant worry on top of Andrew's war experiences had made her husband ill: 'But it need not have come to this. In civvy street we could have gone to our trade union, or Member of Parliament. In the Services you are not supposed to talk to anyone outside.'

In 1982 the British government paid £1,000 under the Criminal Injuries Act to a woman who suffered from severe shock when she saw her husband's unoccupied car blown up outside their home in Northern Ireland. What price would they have put on Christopher White's experiences in the Falklands if he had been a civilian? Christopher tried to commit suicide twice because of his experiences on the exploding *Sir Galahad*. He returned home physically intact with a ship's landing pass pinned to him, recording the diagnosis of battle shock. It was four months before he was given 'light duties' with his battalion, months in which his wife and family anxiously, lovingly, and with no professional guidance nursed him back to some semblance of normality. In 1983 the young Marine, whose life Christopher White had saved, was paid £75,000 by the South Atlantic Fund for the loss of his leg. What price the loss, even temporarily, of Christopher's mind? – £500.

Christopher's 1st Raiding Squadron Royal Marines were among the first ashore at San Carlos Bay on 21 May 1982. As the coxswain of one of the rigid raiding craft – a seventeen foot open boat with a forty horse power outboard engine, giving a top speed of thirty knots – he spent the next two weeks running a 'glorified taxi service', ferrying personnel and equipment between the task force ships and shore-based camps. The boats were frequently under air attack and strafing by Argentine planes. During one bombing raid in the Ajax Bay area Chris was about to go ashore when he first heard, and then saw, two bombs fall within splashing distance of his boat. Drenched by their sea spray, he waited for the inevitable – *both* bombs failed to explode. After the sinking of the *Sheffield* on 4 May, Chris had written to his wife asking her to send him a good luck charm and she had brought a St Christopher medallion, had it blessed by a priest, and mailed it to him. He was wearing it the day the bombs did not detonate, and again when he was the only man left alive *and* intact in his section of the *Sir Galahad*.

Chris and a colleague were detailed to take their boats to the landing ship *Sir Galahad* to move men and equipment for the final push into Stanley. They were pleased to be on board a dry, warm ship after four weeks sleeping rough in an old slaughter house on the San Carlos beachhead. They not only had a good night's sleep in a dry bunk, but a hot meal and hot shower. On the morning of 8 June the *Sir Galahad* was at anchor in Bluff Cove. Chris was in the recreation area on a lower deck when, just after 1 pm, two Mirages and two Skyhawks streaked across the sky and the first of four 1,000 pound bombs hit the ship, which, within seconds, was ablaze.

Chris struggled to his feet in the smoke-filled, pitch black deck, amazed he was still alive and in one piece. Nobody else appeared to be. Then he heard someone shouting for help. Their calls to each other guided Chris through the debris, smoke and gaping holes to Kevin Woodford, a twenty-two-year-old Royal Marine who had been put aboard the *Sir Galahad* because he had trench foot. Kevin had been bending over his backpack reaching for some notepaper to write a letter home when the bomb exploded. When he tried to sit upright he realised he had lost the lower part of his left leg. He later told me: 'It was dark, there was this choking smoke and the smell of fire. I could not see or hear anybody and I did not know which way to crawl. I shouted and Chris answered, and my shouts guided him through the smoke.' Chris half-dragged, half-lifted him out of the immediate area, but, weakened by the smoke and Kevin's weight, could not get him to the upper deck.

Kevin remembers Chris saying he would have to get help. He could now feel the heat from the fire and thought no one would find him in time. He started to push himself along on his hands when two men with torches found him and carried him out on deck: 'Chris had told them where to find me and stayed on deck to recover from the smoke and help the fire fighting team. Just as the helicopter lifted me off the ship there was a big explosion. I must have lived nine lives in ten minutes.'

Chris White still cannot remember what really happened after he left Kevin to find help. Before his transfer to the hospital ship *Uganda* he stole a loaded pistol, which was gently coaxed from him after he spoke of taking his life. On the *Uganda* he injected himself with morphine. He would not speak to anybody or answer their question, why, after surviving such a horrific ordeal, he did not want to live. It was the ship's padre, talking to other *Sir Galahad* survivors and Kevin, who was in intensive care, who guessed what might have happened. He took Chris to see Kevin, who said of that meeting: 'I do not know who cried the most, him or me. He had saved my life.' But Chris, because he had not found Kevin among the ship's survivors in the general ward, had thought him dead and blamed himself for not having got him to safety.

When Chris was allowed home to convalesce, the staff at the Royal Navy hospital, Plymouth, warned his wife that if he had a relapse he would have to go back to hospital immediately. Gillian said no one told her what symptoms to look for, what behaviour to expect; her only clue to his condition had been the diagnosis scribbled on a passenger's landing pass. She knew nothing more until Chris hesitantly, and piecemeal, recounted what he allowed himself to remember.

Gillian continued with her work at Bristol University to help pay the mortgage on the house she had moved into with their son Daniel while Chris was in the Falklands. Chris started to decorate their new home, while someone from his or Gillian's family kept him company during the day. Gillian describes those months as 'physically and mentally draining on both of us'. Her husband's behaviour was unpredictable; there were periods of depression and elation, silence and long monologues; he started to chain-smoke and drink more than he had before going to the Falklands. Some nights he could not sleep, on others he sleepwalked. His memory played tricks, he forgot where he put things or what he had just said or done. On one of their infrequent out-patient visits to Plymouth, Gillian was asked, in front of her husband, how she thought he was coping. She told me: 'If I had any doubts I would never have spoken of them in front of Chris and undermined his increasing self-confidence.'

Gillian is an intelligent, articulate young woman who was desperate to know how to help her husband return to his former, cheerful self. He is a good-looking, smartly dressed, friendly, twenty-seven-year-old, who had taken great pride in being a Royal Marine and, during those weeks in the South Atlantic, proved himself a fearless soldier. His reaction to Kevin's cry for help speaks for itself. His wife will never forgive a system that, at the time she needed help and guidance, gave none. A system that refused adequately to compensate her husband for what she calls 'the scars on his mind. People can see when a man has lost an arm or a leg, but nobody can see what a war does to a man's mind. I think my husband deserves something more for what he has been through.'

Chris returned to light duties with his Plymouth-based squadron in October and insisted on going with them to Northern Ireland the following February. His wife said he 'wanted to prove to himself and his mates he was really better'. Chris told me he also thought it might help his application to join the police force, as he believed what had happened to him after the *Sir Galahad* bombing would be held against him by future employers who needed to see his medical record. He was also aware there was a feeling among some of his senior officers that he had been shaken up a bit but should now pull himself together. The Royal Marines are an elite corps; it was not the done thing to crack up. But his fellow soldiers, who knew what had happened to him in the Falklands: 'Mothered me, got me drunk, kept an eye on me. And I was excused fire drill.' He had planned to leave the Marines that summer, rather than sign on for another

130

minimum five years, and the Falklands War had reaffirmed his decision. He was rattled by the events that had led to the tragedy on the *Sir Galahad*: 'I am professional enough to know how to take care of myself as a soldier but I am not fire-proof and I am bitter that someone was responsible for that dreadful mistake.'

While in Northern Ireland Chris met a Marine who had received £10,000 from the South Atlantic Fund for a flesh wound – a bullet had passed through the back of both legs – and who returned to full duties weeks before Chris. But, when I asked Captain Anthony Lambourne, the secretary of the South Atlantic Fund, about payments to battle-shocked soldiers, he replied: 'This is a delicate subject and a very grey area. Payments will be totally dependent on medical advice and recommendation. One of the questions might be "What about those men who carried on?" ' The value judgement behind such a remark is reminiscent of a military that used to shoot soldiers because they no longer wished to take part in war, a military that pinned medals on limbless heroes and ignored what war had done to men's minds. In December 1982 I had spoken to Alf Morris about the Fund's attitude to soldiers like Chris and in a written reply to his question, Jerry Wiggin told him: 'A total of 30 Servicemen are still receiving some form of in-patient or out-patient psychiatric treatment as a result of their experience in the South Atlantic; of these only one had also suffered a physical injury. The South Atlantic Fund is administered to serve the needs of all who suffered from the campaign, including those who have developed psychiatric complaints.' I forwarded a copy of this reply to the Fund. On 17 December the Whites received £300 to cover their travel expenses for hospital visits. At the end of January 1983 they got an interim payment of £500 from the Fund – at least it was a precedent. But eight months later they were told there would be nothing more.

Chris was not medically discharged. He was due to complete his ten years' service with the Royal Marines in the summer of 1983. He was no longer receiving psychiatric treatment when he left, having returned to normal duties. When his application to join the police force was rejected, he decided that, given his recent medical history and local unemployment, he would be his own boss and work as an insurance agent.

Gillian said he could not have chosen a more high-pressure job, but she felt he had to find his own level and she did not know where to draw the line. Chris needed the family car during the day for his induction course with a local insurance agency, and later for visiting potential customers. It meant driving Gillian to work (there was no convenient public transport), dropping Daniel off at nursery school, returning for him at lunchtime to take him to a child-minder, until teatime, when Chris picked him up on his way to collect Gillian. Chris found it increasingly difficult to juggle the time needed to build up his own business – his first work experience in civvy street – on top of running his family around. It was also costing them £80 a month in petrol. Something had to go. Gillian's doctor advised her to give up her job. Not long after, Chris realised he had been over optimistic in the middle of a recession about earning a realistic wage from selling insurance. He began to look for a permanent job – he is still looking. His wife, who at first did not know what symptoms to look for when he came home to convalesce, is familiar enough with them now.

Almost two years after the war Chris was unemployed, he had sold his South Atlantic campaign medal for £100 to help pay household bills, he had recurrent bouts of depression, sleepwalking and loss of memory. Gillian said he is still one-third of a different person from the man she had known for six years: 'He is a marvellous man who, through no fault of his own, is now unemployed and worried sick about our future as a family. I no longer know how to deal with what is happening to us.'

Chris and Kevin have not met since their return to England. When I visited Kevin at the house he had just moved to in Loughborough with his wife Angela, the first thing he said to me was: 'Did Chris get a medal or something? He deserved it.' When I told him what had happened to the White family, this football-mad young man, who had been a bricklayer before joining the Marines and, eighteen months later, lost a leg in the Falklands War, responded with a compassion that would have put to shame the desk-bound trustees of the South Atlantic Fund, and the officers who felt Chris should pull himself together. Kevin was buying his own, modern, new house with money from the Fund; parked outside was a £6,500 Triumph Acclaim, a present from an appeal fund set up by the villagers of Keyworth, Notts, where Kevin had lived with his parents before going to the Falklands. He had just started work as a clerk at the Midlands Electricity Board, who had decided to give job priority to local injured Falklands veterans.

Kevin was appreciative of everyone who had helped him, but also aware that without the generosity of the Keyworth villagers he would have been housebound, as his parents did not have a car and he needed transport to accept the six-month rehabilitation course he had just completed with the Electricity Board. Without the money from a public charity, Kevin and Angela would have been unable to start their married life in their own home. Kevin thought it grossly unfair that Chris had not been given any similar help: 'Surely his "illness" put him back as much as me in a way.' Like the soldiers who had 'mothered' Chris on his return to duty with his squadron, Kevin is a different generation from the men appointed by John Nott to run the Fund, a set-up described by one unemployed, wounded veteran as 'a Whitehall job creation programme'. These young men would never define the needs of a shell-shocked soldier as a 'grey area'.

Surgeon Commander Morgan O'Connell, the Royal Navy psychiatrist who went to the Falklands with the task force, told me he was having difficulties compiling a dossier of cases of Servicemen who had received, or were still receiving, psychiatric treatment. He was concerned about those who had left the Services and might be suffering from the delayed effects of their war experiences. He believed the attitude of the South Atlantic Fund to be 'outdated', and welcomed any attempt to publicise the issue. But who ultimately will be responsible for the financial and welfare needs of the unidentified men Commander O'Connell is so concerned about in a society that turns away from those that are known to them? Will it be, as in the past, left to charities like the Ex-Services Mental Welfare Society, whose recent campaign poster read: 'Some of the worse wounds are the ones that don't show. It used to be called shell-shock. Now we know more.' We may now know more about mental anguish, but do we *really* care more?

In November 1983 the Director of Army Psychiatry would

not give a figure, but conceded that a 'tiny' number of task force casualties were still being treated. What proportion of a 28,000 strong task force constitutes a tiny number? Jerry Wiggin is the Whites' local MP. Gillian wrote to him about the South Atlantic Fund's refusal to pay compensation to her husband. She received an acknowledgement on 1 November 1983 that he would make some inquiries, but heard nothing more. That same month, the *Guardian* detailed the case of a Fleet Chief Petty Officer who had been in the Navy for twenty-two years and suffered a nervous breakdown after he returned from the Falklands War. He was eventually medically discharged, and the Department of Health and Social Security, in awarding him a fifty per cent disablement pension of £27.52 a week, stated in a letter: 'We have considered your claim to a disablement pension and we have decided that your condition, nervous breakdown, can be accepted as attributable to service.' The South Atlantic Fund refused to pay him a penny.

Months after their return home, injured soldiers spoke to me about their worries for the future, and how, as disabled men in civvy street, with unemployment at record levels, they would provide for their families if they were medically discharged from the Services. At a 1982 Christmas party at Chelsea Barracks, an officer of the 2nd Battalion Scots Guards said to his men: 'It is a shame that it takes wives to do something about changing the Army rule book.' He was referring to the stoppage of the London living allowance. It was a social occasion and the soldiers were too polite to tell him it was a shame their officers had done nothing about changing a rule that penalised men for being wounded in war. The dismissive attitudes to the Falklands injured, who were offered so little help and kept so long in the dark about their futures, had quite an impact on other Servicemen who witnessed their hole-in-the-wall treatment. For a while, the atmosphere at Chelsea Barracks, Pirbright camp and Aldershot completely changed after the war. Men who had not been injured wondered how their own families would have managed if they had been wounded or killed. In some battalions there were temporary, but serious, discipline problems. The war had left many then cynical, distrustful of authority, and angry at the way some of their wounded colleagues were being treated. Their opinions were reinforced by the action of some of the injured Servicemen's wives, who insisted their husbands leave the Services rather than stay on in clerical or storekeeping jobs with little prospect of promotion. They were prepared to risk unemployment rather than continue to live under a system they felt had treated them so shabbily.

Almost two years after the war those worries remained. Many had received enough money from a public charity to buy their own homes, and provide for their immediate needs. Others, like Andrew Wallis and Chris White, did not know how their lives – so unexpectedly changed by an unforeseen war – would turn out. Soldiering is the profession of young men. What will become of these Falkland veterans – particularly those still receiving medical care for their injuries – in twenty or thirty years time? Will they still be dependent on State handouts, topped up by means-tested gifts from public charities? And will their widows, like those of men wounded in the Second World War, still have to go before a DHSS tribunal to prove their husbands eventually died of their injuries, before they can receive a war widow's pension?

The brevity of the Falklands War, the mercifully low casualty figures, the belated cash payments from a public charity, pre-empted many of these questions. But, given the tardy response of the Services to the needs of the injured when they first returned home, the penal attitude behind the withdrawal of their allowances because they were not fit for duty, and the lack of interest by the civil authorities, it is not too early to begin asking them now.

At the end of 1983, of the 578 Servicemen who had been treated for injuries ranging from trench foot to amputations, forty three were still receiving hospital care and seventeen had been medically discharged from the Services. The *Sir Galahad* casualties, such as Welsh Guardsman Simon Weston, who, with forty six per cent burns, was the most badly injured Falklands veteran, will continue their treatment for some years. His family have nothing but praise for the skill of the staff at Queen Elizabeth Military Hospital, Woolwich. His mother, Pauline Hatfield, told me the attention her son had received had been: 'Second to none. If young men had to be injured like this, there is nothing better for them than the

Woolwich.' As an experienced district nurse, Pauline knew what questions to ask the Army doctors about Simon's treatment and the Woolwich medical team had always answered. She said his surgeon, Colonel McDermot, had never said 'if' or 'maybe', but always laid it on the line and, by that same token, she had insisted they be honest with Simon: 'But all the time I think of the future, and what will happen when he leaves the Army. I let them know how deeply we care and how they cannot get away with anything.'

But who takes care of the carers?

The Hatfields are part of a traditional extended Welsh family. Simon's sister, aunts and grandparents live in or near the village of Nelson, mid-Glamorgan. Right from the start, the family, and the local community, have rooted for Simon's recovery. Their collective concern has been an invaluable part of his personal determination to confound the original medical opinion that he would not live. The local butcher pinned progress bulletins on Simon in his shop window, with the hospital's address for people to send letters and cards. In the first year after her son returned home, Pauline visited him laden with gifts from the village – freshly pressed ham the butcher had cooked for him, tins of salmon people gave her in the street, packs of soft drinks given by the grocery shop. Simon had been the first schoolboy of his age group in Nelson to join the Welsh Guards. When he left for the Falklands, four months before his twenty-first birthday, he was fifteen-and-a-half stone of pure muscle, as fit as a Welsh rugby champion. His mother proudly described him as a soldier through and through, and nothing like the public image of Guardsmen as ceremonial troops, or 'Wooden Tops': 'He went to Ireland when he was eighteen. I would not have been bitter then, or later, had he died. It was what he wanted to do.' But when he came home the weekend before he left for the Falklands, the South Atlantic was the last place he wanted to go, although he could not explain why.

The family's active involvement in Simon's hospital treatments has been a vital part of his long-term recovery. It has meant a rota of family visits, and staying as paying guests in hospital accommodation at weekends. The expense of that voluntary care is something Pauline would prefer to ignore, if she had been able to afford to do so. The family refused to touch a penny of Simon's South Atlantic Fund money, insisting it is the only future he has, and must last him for the rest of his life. Pauline works full-time, her husband is retired. During those eleven months after Simon returned home, Pauline made the journey from Nelson to Woolwich forty-five times. It is 188.4 miles from her front door to the hospital, a round trip which cost £27.34p for petrol. The hospital accommodation was £7 a night, their canteen meals 68p for lunch, £1.21 for dinner. When her husband stayed with her they tried to economise by skipping the midday meal and taking their own provisions, like tea, milk and coffee, sometimes boiling eggs in a kettle. When Simon came home to Nelson for his birthday on 7 August – a month after he had returned from the Falklands wrapped like a parcel in rubber foam – it was his mother who brought him home, and drove him back after the weekend. No one had offered alternative transport. It was she who creamed his burns and changed his dressings, and the bedding he used that weekend had to be completely replaced.

Pauline told me how, financially, they could have coped with the additional costs, if it had been a temporary emergency, but Simon needed – and still needs – long-term care, and her place was at his side. It reached the point where the family savings had dwindled. Simon's injuries had been a totally unforeseen event in their lives, and that year they had decided to buy their council house, installed French windows to the carefully tended walled garden, and bought a new car, which was essential to Pauline's work.

With all the publicity the *Sir Galahad* and the Welsh Guardsmen received it was to be expected that someone would eventually call on the Hatfields and see if they could help in any way. Pauline remembered how a woman from SSAFA came a couple of times, and said she *might* be able to get some help with their telephone bill: 'One day she upset me so much with her attitude I cried, and said "Please go away"; I felt like a leech on society.' The SAAFA woman asked a British Legion representative to visit them. Pauline told me: 'The man said he could only spend up to £20 cash, but he could get me a new pair of shoes if I needed. What did he think we were? I did not want a pair of shoes. He then said he could get me a ton of coal. I told him, what do I want with coal?' He had come to Nelson on the bus; when Pauline offered him a lift, he asked to be dropped off at his local pub; she did so and never heard from him again.

The last time she had seen the Welsh Guards' liaison officer at Maindy Barracks, during the days she desperately sought news of her son, she had asked what arrangements there might be for her to stay with Simon at his hospital when he returned. She remembers how he had promised to find out, and added that should she need any financial help the regiment had 'a little available, all I had to do was ask'. She had never asked for anything like that in her life; she could not bring herself to ask. It was her husband who eventually rang the Welsh Guards, who sent a cheque for £100 to cover the cost of their three journeys, two of them abortive, to RAF Brize Norton to meet Simon's plane. Despite the regularity of the Hatfields' visits to Woolwich, they had to phone the Welsh Guards each time they needed their travel expenses reimbursed. Pauline could not stay in the house when her husband made those calls. She showed me all the petrol receipts she had kept from those journeys: 'Just in case someone comes along and accuses me of spending the money on a pair of curtains.'

Simon's rehabilitation would not have been so successful without the care lavished on him by his family and a stream of his friends, who called at the Hatfield house to keep him company, take him to the pub, local working men's clubs, and rugby matches. When Pauline was at work, the constant attention he needed in his first months at home was given by his retired step-father, who cooked his meals, fed him, helped him bath and dress, during the painful weeks when he could not use his own still healing hands. On one occasion Pauline's husband, who had just returned from hospital himself after a prostate operation, felt unwell and asked Simon to pour him a whisky. Simon's fingers could not cope with opening the bottle. When Pauline came home, her son was furious with her for not having been there when they both needed her. But her job was an essential part of their income; she needed to work and, with her husband at home, no one had approached them about domiciliary help.

In March 1983, after a reminder to the Welsh Guards from Pauline's husband that no one, other than an Army padre, had visited them since 13 June 1982, when the liaison officer had told them Simon was dying, Captain Brian Morgan called. He said they were going to withdraw financial support because they did not want the families to become too dependent on the regiment. He had not realised that the only transport that Simon ever had from the hospital to his home was that provided by his family. For the first time since his return from the Falklands War, the Welsh Guards arranged Simon's transport, and have continued to do so.

Sixteen months after the end of the war, Pauline met Simon's platoon commander. He asked her if there was anything they could do for the family. She told him: 'You are too late.'

CHAPTER SEVEN:

The Families visit the Falklands

'I came home from the Falklands finally knowing Matthew was dead and full of bitterness at the waste of it all.' Janet Stuart, whose son died on his eighteenth birthday.

The Christmas after Andy died his widow, June Evans, resigned from her job to spend more time with her two children. They were familiar with their father's absences because of his work, but the realisation that this time he was not coming home upset them very much. Mark had been confused and hurt when his classmates would not at first believe him when he told them his father had been killed in the Falklands. He looked forward to the government sponsored families' visit to the islands in April, although his younger sister, Samantha, insisted on staying at home. For June, it was a journey she had to take before she could make any decisions about the future. She had many times tried to imagine how it might have been for her husband the morning he was killed. She could recite the detailed description Andy's co-pilot had given her, and the pictures she had seen in the newspapers and on the television had given it substance. She told me: 'I could really imagine the sea, the helicopter, the place they went ashore, and the farmhouse.' But she needed to see it for herself in the hope that once she had confirmed the minutiae she could put it to the back of her mind.

There was something else – she wanted to meet the Falkland farmer's family who had sheltered and comforted her critically wounded husband. The farmer's wife, Colleen Ford, had read an interview I had done for the *Sunday Mirror* with June. She had then written to June to say how she had thought of her when Andy's co-pilot had told them of his colleague's wife and children. The Fords, who had two sons the same age as June's children, had sheltered a seventeen-year-old islander, John Thain, during the Argentine occupation of Stanley, his home town. John had helped Andy's co-pilot bring him ashore to the farmhouse and he, too, wrote to June to say how sorry they were they had not been able to do more. He told her how his late father, a Scotsman from Aberdeen, had captained the Falkland Island Company ship, the *Monsunen*, on which he was now a crewman, and enclosed Falkland postcards and stamps for Mark.

June was not bitter that her husband had died doing the only job he ever wanted to do, and knowing that he had been with people who cared, people he was fighting for, had made it a little easier. The Evans had had a good marriage; together they had achieved all the ambitions Andy had set for himself before his thirtieth birthday – to have children, their own home, his helicopter pilot's licence. His wife had always been aware of the risks involved in his work, but Andy was so confident she had believed him indestructible, and for it to end in such an unimagined way was difficult to come to terms with. Their relationship was such that she had expected if anything had happened to either of them the other would be there, 'to hold your hand, and, because the farmer's wife took my place when Andy was dying, I had to meet her'.

The day before June left for the Falklands she walked to the village churchyard to lay Spring flowers on the grey Cornish granite memorial to a man who was buried in the South Atlantic from the deck of a war-requisitioned Cunard cruise liner. Etched on the plaque were the words: 'Andrew Peter Evans 1949–1982. He lived and died bravely that others might live freely.' It was almost a year after Andy had left to go to war that his widow and son flew to Montevideo, where they boarded another Cunard liner, the *Countess*, for the remaining 1,200 miles to the Falkland Islands.

The visit had been arranged by the Ministry of Defence under a scheme introduced by the government in the late Sixties for facility trips by the next-of-kin to the graves of Servicemen killed abroad. Sixty-four families had asked that their men be brought back to Britain for reburial and those families were not eligible for the visit. The 500 relatives – widows and their children, parents of single men, and their brothers and sisters – who boarded the two British Airways flights on 5 April 1983 would visit the remaining graves and memorials to the 255 casualties, including those who had been lost and buried at sea. The arrangements for the visit were not without the usual range of human dramas; there were domestic squabbles about which next-of-kin could, or could not, go, how many members of each family – particularly those grown in number by divorce and remarriage – were eligible for the journey, and, where invitations were declined, a last minute scramble for whatever berths were left on the ship.

The motives for making such an emotional journey, which coincided with the war's first anniversary, were as mixed as the bereaved families' feelings about the war. For Lynda Gallagher it was a personal attempt to find out why the war had happened and what Lawrence had actually died for. She was not satisfied with the explanations of politicians, and hoped to discover something at first hand. To her, the war had seemed a farce, a needless tragedy in which more men had been killed and injured than the total population of the islands. Although Lawrence might have died as he wished, fighting for his Queen and country, she could never look at it that way. After the war, she remembered talking to some Cockneys who were working on a building-site in Hereford, for whom the war had been just like another television serial. It had not affected their lives one bit, and they had no opinions or feelings about it.

Some families, including elderly parents, had never flown before, never mind take a twenty-hour flight to be followed by an immediate transfer to a sea-going ship. One mother said she had dreaded the visit but felt it was her duty – in the same way that she had taken her son to school on his first day, she had to trace his last journey too. Another, whose son had died on his eighteenth birthday, expressed what many, fleetingly, thought. She had to go to the Falklands to face up to the reality of her son's death. At the back of her mind she set out half expecting him to be waiting for her in Port Stanley. Many sought confirmation of how their sons and husbands had died. Marion Pryce craved every detail of her son's last minutes, no matter how painful. She had already discovered from the Servicemen she had spoken to on their return to England that her son had lowered himself from the *Atlantic Conveyor* down a ladder into the sea. His lifejacket had been correctly inflated by two-thirds, but when he was picked up twenty minutes later it had deflated, and he had drowned. His body had been taken on board the *Alacrity* at the same time as that of Frank Foulkes, whose wife Dorothy had only been able to piece together the last minutes of her husband's life from the details Marion Pryce had given her.

Cunard had continued to insist that they did not know how their crewmen had died, and Dorothy hoped that she, too, might discover more by going to the South Atlantic. Despite the personal account of the ship's destruction given her by the *Atlantic Conveyor*'s doctor, she was still not sure what to believe. People had given her the impression that Frank had died fire-fighting, trying to save lives, but when she checked with other families they had been told the same story about their men. For months her youngest daughter had had nightmares thinking of her father trapped in the ship's fire. Cunard had returned Frank's personal possessions in a plastic bag strewn with tobacco from his pipe. His cap, still wet with sea-water, his tobacco tin, a gold pen and pencil set she had given him and his wedding ring showed no signs of having been in a fire. She was upset they had removed the ring before his sea burial; 'he had never taken it off in the twenty-nine years we had been married, and to have it taken from him then was very upsetting.' But at least whenever her daughter dreamt her father was trapped by the ship's fire Dorothy could reassure her by bringing out Frank's things.

There were widows who were grateful for the opportunity the Falklands visit gave them to show their children where their fathers had died, as being on the spot made it easier for them to explain what had happened. One said her husband had been a very patriotic man who had worshipped the Royal family, Britain and the Royal Navy. When he was killed his name and photograph had been in all the newspapers, and their children had proudly shown their schoolfriends and neighbours. Whatever her own feelings about the war, she felt she could not deny her children their belief that their father was a hero.

One widow described to me how the tension, heightened by grief as the ship approached the islands, was palpable and, when triggered by tiredness and seasickness, explosive. She remembered there were a lot of family upsets: one divorced couple quarrelled throughout the trip because the wife blamed the ex-husband for their son's death, all the family had been in the same regiment and the boy had felt obliged to join them too because of the family tradition. Other passengers were upset by those who appeared to treat the journey like a holiday and complained that, having come all that way, they were not spending enough time ashore sightseeing. During the four days they were in the Falklands, they disembarked only for the various memorial services and visits to the homes of those islanders in the Stanley area who had asked to entertain them. Some parents disapproved of the occasional high spirits of a few young widows, who had been briefly married before their husbands were killed, and of those who rushed on to the sun-deck in their bikinis on the one day the sun appeared on the return voyage to Montevideo.

But there were those who rarely left their cabins, unable to share their grief. Others found it comforting to do so, particularly many of the parents; this was the first opportunity they had had of spending time with others who, like themselves, had felt alienated from the unfamiliar world of the Services in which their sons had given their lives. Their conversations led to the formation of the Association of Parents of Unmarried Sons and another group, the Falkland Families Association, which was open to anyone who wished to go on future visits to the islands.

To many of the passengers on the Cunard *Countess*, the islands were nothing like they had expected. Port Stanley had looked like a shanty town from the sea, and close up it was not much better. Some heard complaints from the islanders at the inconvenience of no longer being able to use Argentine hospitals, or have the option of sending their children on to higher education on what they referred to as 'the mainland'. An elderly couple in Port Stanley told the parents of a Royal Navy officer that if they had been younger they would have left. The war, the size of the British garrison, and their uncertain future, had completely changed their way of life and they just hoped that some arrangement could be quickly reached with the Argentines, as they were more familiar with dealing with them than the British.

Such sentiments did not endear them to the visiting families, although Pat and Leslie Stockwell sympathised with those who were honest enough to express their opinions. They had felt no bitterness towards the Argentines; indeed, they had admired the bravery and skill of the young Argentine airmen during the war. Their visit rekindled the anger they had felt at the sinking of the *Belgrano*. They told me how horrified they had been that the war cabinet, having declared an exclusion zone, then changed the rules. They believed that if only the Argentines had been allowed more time to find a face-saving solution, their son would still be alive.

For Marion Pryce's husband, Don, the journey held personal memories of his visits to the Falklands in the late Sixties as an engineer on the British patrol ship, HMS *Protector*. Don remembered how he had not been allowed into the Colonial Club in Port Stanley, which admitted only officers and certain Falkland families. He said he noted that the same place existed and that his son, not being an officer, would also have been ineligible, 'and yet he gave his life for those people to go on living like that'. Marion returned home with no further details of their son's death, but, having visited the islands, knew she could never again vote for a woman who had failed to prevent such a needless war. Dorothy Foulkes went back feeling that Frank had not died in the name of freedom, but for Britain's pride, and that if the islanders wished to remain British they should live in Britain and have done with it, rather than the government spending millions of pounds protecting a way of life that, after the war, was irretrievable. Pat Stockwell told me that she had hoped their visit would help them come to terms with their grief, but two years after the war she said: 'I feel ashamed that I still can't get over it. Even the joy of our daughter's child, our first grandson, who was born almost a year after Geoff died, is spoilt by the thought of how much Geoff would have loved him.'

The visit confirmed Lynda Gallagher's suspicions that the war should never have happened, but she returned comforted from visiting the place where her husband's helicopter had crashed into the sea. A Hercules flew the SAS families over the exact spot; there was a brief service as the plane dipped and circled over the water, and Lynda recalled the South Atlantic was as still as a millpond: 'As though they were showing us they were at peace, and it gave me some peace of mind too.'

For June Evans, the journey was the catharsis she had sought. Before leaving for the Falklands she had met someone she occasionally went out with, but had been unable to make any decisions about the future until she was sure of her feelings about the past. She had felt self-conscious about her new relationship. People had asked if she felt 'better', as though widowhood was an illness from which she would eventually recover, and she told me there were times when she wondered if she would for ever be known as the Falklands War widow, rather than a person in her own right, 'whoever that might be'. On her return home she did not volunteer anything of her meeting with the farmer's wife and his family, who had comforted her dying husband, and I could not ask. But soon after coming back she left the village where she and Andy had lived, for a new life with the man who had waited for her, not daring to predict how it might be for them on her return.

How do some of the widows who did not go to the Falklands now feel about the war? Maureen Emly had a letter dated 20 June 1983, time 8.45 am. It was written by her husband's Captain, Sam Salt, after casting a dozen red silk roses into the South Atlantic near the spot where the *Sheffield* had gone down the year before. The roses had been sent to Maureen by her husband, Richard, on the birth of their son, and she had given them to Sam before he embarked for a return journey to the islands on a new ship. He wrote to tell her that, although attendance at the brief service for Richard had been voluntary, practically all the ship's company had come up on deck that morning. Maureen had seen no point in going to the Falklands; she was so convinced the Argentines' claim to the islands would eventually have to be accepted by Britain, she would not have known how to explain to her son why his father had died. For months after the war she had been unable to switch on the television and had avoided all newspaper reports of victory celebrations and parades. Her home held few memories of her life with Richard, who had left on an extended sea voyage soon after they moved in. It was not a difficult decision to sell up and move on; creating a succession of new homes during her twelve years of marriage had become a familiar way of life. This time, Maureen decided to live abroad; she needed to distance herself from a country whose government, she felt, had been responsible for such a needless war. She had discussed the move with her sister Pat, who was also a widow, and they had decided that their only priority was Matthew's future and, having satisfied themselves about suitable schools in the place they had chosen to live, they left England.

Maureen's quandary about what to tell her son is shared by widows whose children were babies, or not even born, when their fathers were killed. Jane Keoghane wonders how she will explain the tragedy of Bluff Cove to her son, when no one had explained it to the fifty-one families who lost their men on the *Sir Galahad*. For a while the demands for an inquiry by the Welsh Guardsmen's next-of-kin were forestalled by meetings with senior officers. When it became obvious that no one was going to authorise a formal inquiry, the requests for more details petered away. Jane felt that naming names would never bring her husband back. But Kevin's death was very different from dying in a battle; the casualty figures might even have been acceptable if they had resulted in a victory or an honourable defeat. She felt Bluff Cove was just a terrible mistake, and an embarrassment to the Welsh Guards. How would she ever explain that to a son whose father had been so proud of his regiment?

It was the same dilemma for Caroline Hailwood, whose husband was a non-combatant member of the *Sir Galahad*'s crew. She told me that as their son gets older she will just try to answer his questions as truthfully as possible, but the anger is there when she criticised the words used in Margaret Thatcher's victory talk of 'our boys'. She said: 'That is my husband she is talking about, and he was not one of her boys, he was not even in the Services.' She was equally vehement about people who refer to her as a one-parent family, insisting they do not smudge over, or forget, that her husband was killed in the Falklands, and that she is a war widow.

The brevity of the Falklands War masked its impact on people's lives. For many people the more they have had time to think and learn about the events leading up to those seventy-four days in the Spring and Summer of 1982, the more preposterous the whole affair appears to be. Many had at first believed in the principle behind sending the task force, but at the end of the war, when they realised what exactly their men had lost lives and limbs for, few women could accept the legitimacy of such an action, even though their men might have viewed it differently.

Marica McKay was not bitter, but sometimes angry that the war ever took place; she reasoned that Britain was no longer a colonial nation and the days were long gone when people living the other side of the world, calling themselves British, could expect their mother country to take care of them. When she knew that the majority of the forty-one bereaved Para families had requested their men's bodies be brought back, she, too, asked that Ian be returned for a military funeral at his regiment's home-base. It was not only because she believed it right he should lie with the men who had died with him, but also because neither she, nor Ian's family, wished him to remain on land they believed the Argentines would eventually occupy.

From the accounts of Ian's bravery his widow knew there was a likelihood of a medal, but not until the last minute did she know it was the Victoria Cross. To her, Ian was doing a job he was very good at and she believed the Falklands War, like many other wars, had its share of unsung heroes.

After the announcement of the two VCs, Marica became a little wary of the motives of people who might want to make social or political capital out of her. On Tuesday 12 October, London's Lord Mayor held a privately funded victory parade for 1,200 task force veterans who marched through the City to Guildhall. The salute was taken by the Mayor, flanked in presidential style by Margaret Thatcher. No member of the Royal family was invited and, initially, the war-wounded were excluded – a decision rescinded only at the last moment after criticism by MPs and Lord Snowdon. When Marica was spotted watching the march pass anonymously from a pavement, she was pressed a number of times to take a place on the Lord Mayor's viewing-stand, but declined. She had been a soldier's wife all her adult life, and she had come to watch her husband's regiment take part in a parade, not to celebrate a war. To have stood in public beside the Prime Minister might be seen as endorsing decisions and sentiments she did not necessarily agree with, although Sara Jones, whose husband was also awarded a posthumous VC, appeared to have no inhibition about her televised appearance on the Conservative Party's conference platform at Brighton that autumn.

Marica has loaned Ian's medal to the Imperial War Museum and, to the horror of some of the members of the Parachute Regiment, had on occasions mentioned that, should the need arise, she would have no qualms about selling it. She said: 'A dead hero is soon forgotten by the public. In twenty years' time it won't mean a thing except to the regiment, where it has already become just another part of their history.'

The process of committing the Falklands War and all its heroes to the pages of history happened even quicker than Marica had predicted. Like all regiments who commemorate their victories with annual dinners, parades and specially designed pieces of mess silver, the Paras, who were the war's front-line troops, were quick to honour their two VCs. Within months of the ceasefire an artist called on Marica to select a photograph of Ian which he could use for a painting based on the action in which Ian had died. It had been commisioned for the officers' mess at Aldershot. Marica heard nothing more until she saw a photograph of the portrait and its presentation ceremony in a local paper. She has not yet been invited to see the original. She also has no idea what design had been chosen for the piece of regimental silver being cast to commemorate the VCs, and it was only by chance she heard of the Ian McKay battalion trophy, presented for the first time last year. On the first anniversary of the war there was a brief service at the Paras camp to which none of the widows was invited, although some, like Marica, live just down the road; in fact, she heard from no one that day.

Marica McKay did not expect any special privileges because her husband was awarded the VC, but other than the wife of Ian's CO, no one has kept in touch: 'It is not that you want to be fussed, but it would be nice to be remembered,' she told me.

It is extraordinary that a society which commemorates its dead heroes with medals and pieces of silver can, at the times when it matters most, such as the first anniversary of death, forget the living. Marica's experience was not uncommon, for even in the 1980s, when a war cabinet was led by Britain's first woman Prime Minister, war was still regarded as men's business. The instant books on the Falklands War were almost exclusively based on the accounts of Servicemen and politicians; civic memorials to the dead were sometimes dedicated without the knowledge of their widows; memorial services sometimes reported and televised without any invitations being extended to the bereaved. The ambivalence many felt about the necessity of the war was evident among those authorities who, only after some pressure, agreed to discreet memorials, but flatly refused to add Falklands War names to the civic rolls of honour for two World Wars.

There are those who have no need of engraved stones, whose memories are enshrined in the untouched bedrooms of young men who left home, never thinking that this was going to be the Real Thing. Theresa Burt is not the only mother who had left her son's room as it was when he last slept there. On Saturdays she still watches the teatime television scores for the Chelsea football team, and puts their match reports in her son's room, together with his pocket money. She has continued her claim for Jason's Army insurance, which his regiment say he never signed for and is aware that some people might interpret her letter-writing and the untouched bedroom as the behaviour of a mother deeply disturbed by her son's death. But she told me: 'I am very sane and very angry, and I do not want people to forget how, and why, my son died.'

CHAPTER EIGHT:

A Time to Think

'The Falklands War should never have been a learning situation; the Services should have been prepared for dealing with the domestic problems of war.' Colonel's wife, Meg Baxter.

In 1982, for the first time since the Suez crisis, an amphibious task force set out to do battle in a conventional-style war. The Armed Forces were as unprepared militarily for such a war as they were for dealing with its domestic consequences. The response to many of the bereaved families and, in particular, to the families of war-wounded men, revealed attitudes that had not changed since the Second World War, and were completely unacceptable to an articulate non-conscript generation who had grown up in a Welfare State.

What no one had predicted was the role women insisted on assuming.

The women's first need, that they be kept in touch with what was happening, was largely ignored by both the military and civilian authorities. In our technologically sophisticated age of simultaneous global satellite communications, the task force families, as well as the media, expected to be given up-to-date reports on the war. The early media coverage added to the anxiety of many task force families, who spent hours switching from one television and radio channel to another in the hope of catching any clues to what was really happening in the South Atlantic. The lack of facts added to the unreality of it all, and did not prepare them for the inevitable consequences of all wars – death and injury.

There is an urgent need for the Armed Forces, and in particular the Royal Navy, to reassess and update their relationship with the media, not only in the interests of the public accountability anyone might legitimately expect of the military in a democratic society, but for the peace of mind of its own Servicemen and their families. If the Services are not voluntarily prepared to take the initiative, then the government must do so, and it most certainly should not be left to the Ministry of Defence, who handled media communications during the Falklands War.

The inability of that Ministry to coordinate even the simplest information, between its desk-bound Whitehall staff and local Service personnel dealing with task force families, was staggering. Time and again the Ministry released press reports on casualties before Service welfare officers had had the opportunity to contact the next-of-kin, or they put out partial press releases on casualties without giving any details, causing thousands of families needless hours of worry. A brief, almost off-the-cuff mention of five ships being hit during the San Carlos Bay landings led to 5,000 anxious telephone calls to one naval inquiry desk alone, while the panic-stricken television announcement by John Nott on the loss of a ship, which was not named until the following afternoon, caused much distress.

After the war, the House of Commons Defence Committee held an inquiry on the Ministry's handling of press coverage, where representatives of the media and military publicly aired their differences. They should have called task force widows, wives and mothers as witnesses, too – for the most damning criticisms came from within the Services themselves, including returning Falklands veterans who were appalled by what their families had been through.

Major Chris McDowall, Royal Marines, who was in England throughout the war, and a keen observer of the media coverage, summarised the feelings of many senior officers in a letter to the Marines magazine, the *Globe and Laurel*. He believed that a long-term major reassessment needed to be made of the Services relationship with the media, and the use of the media as a military and political weapon. Some of the questions he posed included: Why was information from the MOD so late, so incomplete and so inaccurate? Why was the military/media interface so resentful? Was it necessary to subject relatives at home to mental suffering by partial press releases? Why did the Army manage to achieve such outstanding PR in comparison with the Naval Services?

The ceasefire made little difference to the Ministry's inept handling of information, except that this time it displayed an insensitive disregard of the feelings of the recently bereaved. For a while, television and newspaper reports from the Falklands still had to be cleared, before transmission or publication, by Ministry minders, who had accompanied the task force journalists. But there seems to have been no attempt to warn the next-of-kin that what they might be about to see on their televisions or read in the next day's newspaper could be distressing. One young widow was alone in her home, for the first time since her return from staying with relatives after her husband had been killed at Goose Green. She accidently switched on a portable television set instead of turning out the bedside light. She was horrified to see a news item about the burial of Goose Green casualties, who were being lowered in body bags into a muddy, communal grave, and actually to hear the padre read out her husband's name. The incident made her more determined than ever to have her husband brought back for reburial. No one bothered to contact widows Dorothy Foulkes or Marica McKay before detailed descriptions of their husbands' deaths appeared in newspapers without them being privately given any similar information.

It was not just the lack of information from the military to the media that caused distress, but the inability of the Armed Forces to communicate with the bereaved families and those who were frantic for news of their injured men. Simon Weston's family sought news of his condition and whereabouts for twenty-four long days. Why were the family of a young man who had lost his leg not told of his arrival until he had been back home twenty-four hours; why was a wife assured her shell-shocked husband was not due home, when his sister had seen him on a television newsreel boarding a plane which arrived the next day? The Armed Forces had few difficulties locating men when they were needed for war; there were no communication problems between the Fleet headquarters at Northwood and the South Atlantic when Margaret Thatcher gave the order to sink the *Belgrano*. After the ceasefire, there was no reason why these resources were not used to keep the families of the injured informed on their condition, whereabouts and arrival home dates. And why did no one from the Services attempt to prepare the families of the war-wounded for coping with their men's injuries?

Weeks after the war ended, my requests for information to the Ministry of what was happening to the widows and wounded were met with hostility and suspicion; requests for possible interviews were ruled totally out of the question. But the self-imposed secrecy and silence of the Services was broken by women whose lives had been completely changed by the war, and who no longer felt constrained by rules that forbade their men to speak openly.

The lack of information from the Ministry and Armed Forces contributed to a highly competitive search by newspapers for 'human-interest' stories about the war. The rush to be first with an 'exclusive' story exposed the murkier practices of the popular press, and on occasions led to legitimate criticism of media harrassment of bereaved families. One journalist tried to pose as a prospective father-to-be in his attempt to visit a hospital maternity ward and gain access to a pregnant war widow. He was rumbled by a nurse who answered his telephone request and recognised his voice from a pervious occasion when he had revealed his real identity. The bitter rivalry between the *Daily Mirror* and the *Sun* newspapers, who had openly criticised each other's coverage of the Falklands War, came to a head with the *Sun*'s claim to have interviewed VC widow Marica McKay. The *Sun* said they spoke to Marica at the home of her parents-in-law in Rotherham but at the time she was in London with *Daily Mirror* journalists, to whom she gave an exclusive interview, for which she refused any payment. The *Sun* newspaper's fabricated 'world exclusive' interview with Marica was later condemned by the Press Council as 'a deplorable insensitive deception on the public.'

The Armed Forces, who had always prided themselves on being a self-sufficient society, were unable to respond adequately to the problems of beareavement. Although only 134 married men were killed the personal touch was often lacking. The insensitive way in which some of the 255 bereaved families received their men's posthumous South Atlantic campaign medals, in pieces, in jiffy bags through the post, is unforgivable.

When it suited them, Service chiefs assembled Falklands veterans for parade-ground presentations of medals by members of the Royal family – surely they could have included the families of the men who had been killed? The penal attitudes to the injured, who had their allowances docked because they were not fit for duty, was reminiscent of an age when the war-wounded were automatically discharged and left to fend for themselves. And yet the government which had sent them to war did little about the welfare of the 777 injured Servicemen, leaving it instead to the Armed Forces and a public charity.

In recent months the Ministry of defence has begun, in some instances, to look at the way it handled the domestic problems and aftermath of the war. There have been meetings between Michael Heseltine and BLESMA representatives whose experience of the problems of ex-Servicemen with amputations was rebuffed by the Ministry when the Falklands War injured returned home.

Perhaps they would care to make up further for inertia by immediately giving disability pensions and mobility allowances to all Servicemen injured in the Falklands who are still in the Armed Forces. It is an untenable anomaly that a soldier who lost a leg cannot claim a disability pension while still in the Services, but a civilian with the same disability, and also fully employed, can do so. It is equally ridiculous that a soldier who lost a leg and now needs a car to get to barracks is not automatically given a tax-free weekly civilian mobility allowance of £19.00 from the DHSS payable to those with severe walking difficulties. This non-payment is certainly a paradox to those Falklands War wounded who were presented with specially adapted cars by the South Atlantic Fund in a belated public relations exercise. Given the fact that the Fund was so cautious about spending its money, and allegedly thoroughly investigated everybody's needs, there can be no question that they did not believe these cars a necessity to the men's mobility. The total cost of automatically giving the mobility allowances to the Falklands War amputees still in the Services would be infinitesimal compared with the government's advanced public spending plans up to 1986 on Fortress Falklands, which will cost £1 million a head for each of the islands' 1,813 inhabitants.

Perhaps war-wounded men have no place in the Armed

155

Forces and, indeed, maybe their continued presence is due only to the predictable public backlash if they had been compulsorily medically discharged. The public outcry would have been even louder if the only money awarded them for their injuries was the pittance the Ministry of Defence are obliged to pay on medical discharge.

The whole issue of insurance and compensation for war-wounded Servicemen needs urgent review, given the differentials paid under the Criminal Injuries Compensation Scheme to soldiers in Northern Ireland. So does the insurance coverage for next-of-kin. It is inexcusable in the 1980s that the inadequacy of statutory provisions had to be made up from the hand-outs of a public charity, with all that implies. There should be a compulsory, State-financed insurance scheme for all Servicemen. The Services have their own in-house schemes which cover all risks, on and off duty, in peace and war. But even after the Falklands War, Service chiefs were very worried about the number of Servicemen still not covered by their own schemes, and the premiums the lower ranks were prepared, or could afford, to pay. As a result of the Falklands War, the Army Dependant Assurance Trust – ADAT – received fifty-three death claims, although 122 Army officers and soldiers were killed. The average tax-free income from those claims was £3,420 a year, but the range of benefits was wide. It was the widows of men from senior ranks, who tended to spend more on insurance, who would receive £750 a month, compared with many ordinary soldiers' dependants receiving just £95 a month.

But it is the Service charities that need the most radical overhaul. They are the repositories for the most conformist attitudes within the Armed Forces, the epitome of an unshakeable, all-male military hierarchy. Their unimaginative administration of the South Atlantic Fund was completely out of touch with the needs and expectations of Servicemen and their families. The running of the Fund was, like everything else to do with the domestic consequences of the Falklands War, left to the Armed Forces and the Ministry of Defence. John Nott's choice of trustees was another cop-out by the government. No war-wounded, no families, no widows, no parents sat in on the charity's deliberations. The assessment panel was totally unrepresentative of the people it was making decisions for,

156

and not accountable to them or to the public who had so generously donated.

It is not surprising that the Fund became a focal point for the anger, grief and bitterness felt by many about the war. The government, which was high on victory and already cashing in on the Falklands Factor, could blatantly ignore any criticism without too much of a backlash from the electorate, and refused to get involved. The Armed Forces, who never engage in public debate, were impotent, and on the rare occasions senior officers publicly criticised the Fund, they were rapidly called into line. The Servicemen and their families were cautioned time and again not to speak to the media about the Fund, or the war, and the threat of the Queen's Regulations was very real – three Welsh Guards were charged and fined for their appearance on a television programme's investigation into the tragedy of Bluff Cove.

The remainder of the Fund should not be distributed willy-nilly among the Service charities for them to hive off into their general purpose funds, but apportioned according to the decisions of a representative sample of the widows, injured and parents. It is really not good enough for the charities to continue to skulk behind outdated laws and insist they cannot administer their finances in any other way. The government's direct involvement in the allocation of money from the Penlee Fund had created a precedent for much greater flexibility.

Unfortunately, the government resisted further pressure to change the charity laws – but, after the upset and confusion caused by the South Atlantic Fund, it should completely overhaul laws which are unacceptable to anyone still dependent on charity because of the inadequacy of State provision.

What will happen in the future when the long-term effects of the war, both physical and mental, take their toll on the Falklands veterans? The current attitudes by the State and charities to those who have suffered shell-shock and had mental breakdowns need urgent consideration, as the delayed effects of the war may not surface for some time. And, in the long run, who will take care of the carers? The belated response to the needs of Simon Weston's family and others does not augur well for the future. And will those widows whose men eventually died of their war wounds, for which they receive disability pensions only after leaving the Services, still have to go before tribunals to prove their deaths were attributable to the Falklands War before they can claim a war widow's pension?

For many women, the strength that has come from sharing a totally unexpected event in their lives has made them more determined to speak up for themselves and their families, and sort these issues out now. Their actions have proved that women no longer regard themselves as 'excess baggage', and will not be content with their exclusively social roles in the Armed Forces. For many, the Services' claim that they take care of their own has lost all credibility. The myths fostered by a family regiment like the Welsh Guards did not stand up to scrutiny, given the experiences of a pregnant war widow and the mother of a severely injured soldier. So it is pleasing to note that, in the Spring of 1984, when Simon Weston had spent weeks at home feeling very low with delayed grief, shock and depression, the Welsh Guards did respond to a request from his family and arranged for him to visit his battalion in Germany. However, when it came down to it, it was the women who took care of themselves, and each other, although the advantages of belonging to a small, highly individual regiment like the SAS, which is socially integrated with a local community, were self-evident. Even for those wives whose husbands returned unharmed from the war, Service life will never be the same again after living through such an unforeseen experience.

Meg Baxter feels that the Falklands taught the Services a lot about dealing with the domestic consequences of war, but they should have been more prepared; it should not have been a learning situation. She said there had been a perceptible change in attitude among those responsible for Service families, but what that would mean in the future remained to be seen. Certainly the initiatives taken by many women could not be ignored, and many now hoped for more involvement in their husbands' careers. Whether that will be allowed depends on the cooperation of the all-male military hierarchy – and some of their wives. Meg's newspaper column was so popular with readers that after the war the editor asked her to write a weekly article on Service life, a decision frowned upon by some senior Service staff, who did not like the public knowing too much about the Armed Forces. Their hostility reached epic proportions when Meg criticised double beds in married quarters for being so uncomfortable. The tabloid newspaper response was very predictable – 'Colonel's wife pans passion killers' were the headlines over photographs of nubile women bouncing up and down on Service bedsprings. The powers that be were not amused – Meg Baxter had really let the side down and was temporarily banned from the officers' wives circle. A salutary tale indeed.

Among the bereaved families I know there is remarkably little bitterness towards the Argentines. Many who went on the next-of-kin visit to the Falklands returned angry at the loss of lives on both sides, and more perplexed than ever at how the British government could have been so inept and lacking in vigilance to have allowed such a war to take place. Widows like Lynda Gallagher accept that for their men the Falklands War was the Real Thing, and they were proud to go and fight for Queen and country. They would not have remained in the Armed Forces if they did not think that way. But in the 1980s women do not always hold the same opinions as their men, and find no comfort in knowing their men thought the war necessary.

The Falklands War also had a profound effect on many young Servicemen who had never imagined they would be engaged in the sort of conflict they had only seen on their television and cinema screens. It will not only be the bereaved who remember.

On the first few occasions a mother and father visited their son's grave in Aldershot's military cemetery, they were puzzled by coins lying in the area, as though someone had scattered a handful of small change. They asked some soldiers what it might mean, and were told their son had been one of a crowd of young Paras who often pooled their small change to buy the last round at a local pub. While they drank, one of them, a ballad singer, would lead them in song. When the Falklands dead were returned for reburial, the young soldiers who had survived their friends would stop off at the cemetery on their way back to barracks from the pub. The singer would lead his drinking companions in a chorus and they would all leave their dead comrades their share of the change for the last round. The ritual ended within a few months. The Falklands veterans had either been posted elsewhere . . . or left the Armed Forces.

The Falklands War 1982

19 March
Argentine scrap-metal workmen land at Leith, South Georgia, to dismantle a whaling station. They hoist the Argentine flag and do not seek authorisation for their presence from the British Antarctic Survey base at nearby Grytviken.

20 March
Margaret Thatcher and the foreign secretary, Lord Carrington, agree to despatch the British survey ship *HMS Endurance*, with twenty Royal Marines aboard, to South Georgia from Port Stanley.

23 March
A dozen Argentines remain at Leith and two days later an Argentine naval supply ship delivers supplies and puts ashore a full marine detachment under Captain Alfredo Astiz.

26 March
The Argentine government says it will give all necessary protection to the workmen.

28 March
The Argentine restates its claim to the Falkland Islands and Dependencies.

1 April
President Ronald Reagan at the request of Margaret Thatcher telephones President Galtieri and urges restraint.

2 April
Argentine invasion of the Falklands.

3 April
Margaret Thatcher announces the despatch of the task force to the South Atlantic.

5 April
The first of 28,000 Servicemen and more than 100 ships leave Portsmouth.

9 April
The war-requisitioned Cunard liner *SS Canberra* leaves South-ampton with 3,000 troops on board.

12 April
A 200-mile maritime exclusion zone is established around the Falkland Islands to prevent Argentine reinforcements and supplies from the mainland.

25 April
South Georgia retaken with the Argentine surrender at Grytviken.

30 April
With the arrival of the task force, the maritime exclusion zone is declared a total exclusion zone, applicable to all ships and aircraft supporting the Argentine occupation of the islands.

2 May
The Argentine cruiser the *General Belgrano* is sunk with the loss of 368 lives outside the total exclusion zone by the British submarine *Conqueror*.

4 May
HMS Sheffield is sunk with the loss of twenty lives.

12 May
The war-requisitioned *QE2* leaves Southampton with the Scots and Welsh Guards on board.

19 May
A Sea King helicopter crashes into the sea with the loss of its crew and nineteen SAS Servicemen.

21 May
San Carlos landings. Two helicopters shot down, five ships damaged, frigate *HMS Ardent* sunk and twenty-two crewmen killed. *HMS Argonaut* damaged and two crewmen killed.

22 May
HMS Antelope damaged by an unexploded bomb and one crewman killed. Later the ship explodes and sinks when bomb disposal officer attempts to defuse the bomb.

25 May
HMS Coventry hit and capsized with the loss of twenty lives. Cunard's transport vessel, the *Atlantic Conveyor*, abandoned after being bombed and set on fire with the loss of twelve lives.

28 May
Battle for Darwin and Goose Green in which Lieutenant–Colonel 'H' Jones of the 2nd Battalion Parachute Regiment is among seventeen soldiers killed.

8 June
Bluff Cove disaster in which the landing ships *Sir Galahad* and *Sir Tristram* are bombed and fifty-one men die including thirty-eight Welsh Guards.

11–12 June
Battle for Port Stanley in which Sergeant Ian McKay of the 3rd Battalion Parachute Regiment is among twenty-three paratroopers killed.

12 June
HMS Glamorgan bombed and thirteen crewmen killed.

14 June
Argentine surrender at Port Stanley.